Undercover Reunion

By

Raven West

ISBN-13: 978-1467995740
ISBN-10: 1467995746

PROLOGUE

"I DON'T WANT TO DIE!"

"Shut up, Chuck. We're not going to die."

If he doesn't quit his whining, I'll kill him myself, Melanie thought as she ran her fingers along the concrete blocks feeling for an opening. "Katie, can you find any cracks on your side of the room?"

"No, Mel. However Wyatt built this place, he made sure whoever or whatever he put in here wouldn't be able to get out."

Katie tried to clear the dust away from an area on the floor next to Eric and Chuck, who had already resigned to their fate several minutes earlier. "I give up," he sighed, slumping down onto the dirty concrete.

"Melanie, you should listen to Katie and take a break," Chuck groaned. "I'm sure Wyatt will be back soon to let us out. He wouldn't seriously leave us in here to suffocate to death."

"I don't know, Chuck," Eric continued to run his fingers over the concrete wall. "That warning shot he fired at the ceiling looked pretty threatening to me. Then he forced us into this windowless room with apparently no means of opening the door from this side."

"If we could even find the door," Katie said.

"Eric, you're overreacting as usual. When that bullet flew over your head, your freckles nearly jumped from your skin," Chuck teased. "Look, I know we've both been part of Wyatt's shady dealings, but I don't think he's capable of cold-blooded murder. I know he bragged about how he tricked us into helping him execute his master plan and that he didn't want to leave any witnesses, blah, blah, blah. He sounded more like an actor reciting lines from a very bad horror movie than making an actual threat. You know how Wyatt liked to play practical jokes in high school. I just can't imagine he'd really want us all dead." Chuck didn't feel as confident as he hoped he sounded.

"Yeah, well when Wyatt pulled that trigger it sure as hell didn't appear that he was joking. He scared the shit out of me," Eric argued. "I'm beginning to think Wyatt is capable of anything. If Katie's hair wasn't white already, I'm sure it would have turned as soon as she heard that thing go off."

Ignoring Eric's insult, Katie tried to reassure the others. "Look, guys. Wyatt may be a lot of things..."

"Like a liar and a blackmailer..." Eric cursed.

"And a manipulative prick..." Chuck added.

"With an ego the size of Montana..." Melanie tried to lighten the mood.

"...and a few small countries," Katie added with a laugh. "But one thing I know for certain is that Wyatt Gaynes is not a murderer."

"I'm not so certain, Katie. He's isn't the same hot jock high school football star wannabe who dated a different cheerleader every month," Eric began.

"Two or three at the same time as I recall," Chuck added through clenched teeth. "And he always managed to get away with it with that fake boyish charm."

"Still jealous, Chuck?" Melanie said, grinning slightly. "While that might have been true once, thirty years can change a man, and not always for the better. One thing I do know about Wyatt, is that every plan he concocted always contained one major flaw, and that includes the construction of this room. All we have to do is find it. Get your lazy ass off the floor and help us look!"

"We've been looking for more than three hours, Mel. I'm telling you, it's hopeless."

"Chuck, the only thing that's hopeless in this room is you. Now I know why your software company nearly went bankrupt. You have no backbone for a challenge."

Insulted for the last time, Chuck brought his paunch-bellied frame to full standing. The bald spot on his head brushed against the three dim light bulbs dangling from the concrete ceiling causing a spotlight to alternately shine on the desperate expressions of his three former classmates' faces.

"Dammit," Chuck cursed, "You sound as if this is all my fault. Eric and I were doing just fine before you girls showed up."

"You're right, Chuck," Eric immediately joined sides with the only other male in the room, "If you and Melanie hadn't interfered with our plans back in the computer room, we wouldn't all be locked in this damn dungeon, running out of air."

"We have plenty of hot air with the two of you blaming us for your predicament," Katie shot back. "At least we're trying to find a way out of here."

"Girl," she said to her friend, "you look exhausted. Ignore these jerks and take a break."

"I think you're right, Katie. We need to conserve our energy. If you two useless men will just be quiet for a few minutes," Melanie gave Chuck and Eric a piercing stare, "I'm taking five."

Melanie leaned against the cold concrete and wiped the sweat from her forehead with her shirt sleeve. The dampness in the cramped space had turned her wavy auburn hair into a wild frizzy rat's nest. Every muscle in her almost fifty-year-old body was on fire from her thwarted attempts to break out of their prison.

Exhausted, she closed her eyes, took a few deep breaths and mentally began replaying the events of the past few days which had led her fellow incarcerates into the dark hole from which there seemed to be no escape.

Although their individual lives had taken them on very diverse paths, they all shared the unfortunate common denominators of possessing a diploma from Abbeyville High School and being caught in the insidious web of Wyatt Gaynes; a web whose epicenter began in the heartland of Minnesota and stretched throughout the European continent trapping everything in its path.

When the undercover agents first approached Melanie and Kathleen the night of their thirtieth reunion party, the women could never have imagined that the innocent spy game they had played against Eric and Chuck nearly four decades ago would become a real life confrontation with one of the most insidious criminal minds of their generation.

Chapter One
Six Months Ago

This program has performed an illegal operation and will be shut down. If the problem persists, contact the program vendor.

"Dammit, not again."

Melanie cursed at the annoying error message on the computer monitor which cut off her instant message in mid-sentence. She clicked the re-set button then went to the kitchen to get a cup of coffee while she waited for the system to re-boot.

One of these days, I'll have to connect to DSL, she thought as the annoying buzzing of the dial-up connection permeated the room. She had been in the middle of a friendly argument with her best friend about their upcoming high school reunion, and Katie's insistence that she attend was starting to wear down her resolve to keep her attendance a secret. When the computer error occurred, she was almost relieved. Melanie didn't want to let Katie know that she had already made up her mind and she wanted her friend to be surprised.

When Katie first began talking about their reunion nearly a year ago, Melanie had no interest in attending. She'd left small town Abbeyville Minnesota, and everything connected to that lifestyle, as soon as she graduated high school and there was no one from her past she was the slightest bit interested in seeing. Then, a few months back she'd received a surprise phone call from another former classmate, Stuart Janns, who had gone on to become a successful movie and theater critic.

Stuart had told her that he was in Los Angeles for the Golden Globes and thought she might like to attend with him. They spent most of the evening talking about, or rather trashing, their old high school class and he eventually convinced her to go to the reunion, if only for the sheer entertainment of making fun of everyone else. Melanie decided she could spend a few days back in her hometown, but it was going to be a quick trip.

When the computer came back on line, Katie had signed off, but not before leaving one final insistent email:

I just got an error message and was booted off. I need the final count by tomorrow. C'mon Mel, I know you'll have a great time. I'm going to put your name on the acceptance list and hope you'll reconsider.

Melanie shut down the computer, momentarily starring at her reflection in the now dark screen. Thirty years since high school and she was pleased that she had managed to keep the sands of time from etching lines into her face without any help from Hollywood's plastic magicians.

It was well past lunchtime and Melanie was still in her underwear. Since Friday was a short taping day, she didn't need to be in the studio until mid-afternoon. Melanie Tyler might have the most recognizable voice on television, but no one knew what she looked like, and that's the way she liked it.

Melanie moved to Los Angeles a week after getting her Abbeyville diploma. Her plan was to hit the ground running as soon as she graduated from U.C.L.A. found an apartment, a job and an agent. The first two items on her list had been fairly easy to obtain, the third proved to be much more difficult. It wasn't long before Melanie discovered she was just one of more than a thousand hopeful wannabe actors in a city that squashed dreams like mudslides crashing down on Pacific Coast Highway.

Her college graduating class was nearly ten times the size of the population of her entire high school. She soon discovered that the diplomas she'd received from both institutions were as worthless as the paper they were printed on.

While she had been able to find small parts as an extra, enough that she finally qualified for a SAG card, the competition for roles was intense. She went on a few cold calls and received several offers from over zealous producers, but she was never willing to take the short cut to stardom via their office sofa. It seemed as if her career train had become derailed before it had even left the station. After six months of rejection, Melanie was ready to pack her bags and return to Minnesota, but fate had other plans.

A month before her apartment lease was up she was invited to a party by a former classmate who had found work at a local radio station. He told her they were looking for someone to record the station's public service announcements and thought Melanie had the perfect voice for the job.

The next day, she went for an audition and recorded the announcement for the A.S.P.C.A, using a wide range of voices and accents. The response had been so successful that she was hired as their spokesperson. Melanie soon discovered that even though she didn't have the anorexic actor-figure in front of the camera, her voice was magic behind a microphone. It wasn't long after that first broadcast her agent was contacted by the producers a new animated family series, the Franklins. After only one audition she landed the part for the female lead and instead of moving back to her house three miles from a Minnesota lake, she moved into a condo across the street from the Pacific Ocean.

All of her co-workers at the animal shelter gave her a going away party, and a cocker spaniel puppy she'd fallen in love with at first sight. Along with the puppy, she also had taken the agency's executive director, who had fallen in love with her at first sight, or so he said when he asked her to marry him. He quit his job as soon as the ink was dry on the marriage license and used Melanie's income to try and produce his own animated series. As it turned out, he was much better dealing with stray animals then he was with human relationships, business or otherwise. Three years later his company, as well as their marriage, ended. He kept the dog. She kept the Santa Monica condo.

Melanie took her coffee into the living room. She found the faded blue and gold yearbook jammed in between some dusty photo albums on her the bookcase. She ran her fingers over the gold embossed seal which read Honor, Integrity, Knowledge, surrounded by the phrase "Let each one find the truth he is seeking" on the cover just below the title Abbeyville, Minnesota Class of 1972.

She sat down on the couch and began flipping through the pages which had yellowed a bit over the years. The black and white faces, hair styles and clothes from that era were quite dated, but the memories were so clear in her mind that she felt as if the pictures were taken yesterday. She paused to read some of the messages that were scribbled over the faces of people she hadn't bothered to stay in touch with over the years. She stopped on the page where the Ts were listed and found her photo. Staring at barely familiar face, Melanie grimaced at her naive foolishness. How could she have ever thought trying to look like everyone else would work for her? She thought. Judging by her photograph, she had bought into the straight hair parted-in-the-middle look of that era. Fortunately, her older more secure self had outgrown the need to conform and now she no longer spent the time, or the money straightening her naturally curly hair. But unlike Katie, who was perfectly happy with her natural color, Melanie's vanity wouldn't allow even one gray one to be seen. It was her only vice, and unlike many in the acting profession, her breasts, nose and fingernails were totally natural. Her light skin tone intensified her deep blue-green eyes which had remained sharp and thankfully glasses free. Her figure had held up extremely well over the years, even if she did have to work at it a bit harder than when she was in high school.

Turning a few more pages she found the picture of her best friend, Kathleen Conner. Melanie and Katie had been classmates and best friends since Kindergarten. The small town of Abbeyville, population 5001, had only one school building which was built on a ten-acre lot. Melanie's older brother had been killed and Katie didn't have any siblings. Consequently, their friendship had developed into a very close sisterly relationship. Melanie read the inscription her girlfriend had written and laughed out loud: I hope you become a great Hollywood actress, and work for U.N.C.L.E on the side.

It reminded her how, in the sixth grade they had played spies from the old television show. They even had a secret room which Melanie had converted from the tornado shelter her parents built in their basement. Every Friday night after the show was over she and Katie would take their notes into the secret room and discuss every detail of each episode. The girls would even create their own adventures, imagining their classmates were THRUSH agents and their teachers were undercover spies.

Those were some fun times, Melanie thought. Stuart might be right. At the very least the thirtieth reunion would be interesting. Stuart promised it would be fun to see how the popular clique had let themselves go once they landed a good husband and several children and how badly the sports jocks had faired over the years. Perhaps after three decades the old wounds of the past would have had enough time to heal, even those which had left permanent scars.

Melanie continued to glance through the rest of the photos, until she found the one of the person who had been on her mind the moment she decided to attend the reunion; Wyatt Gaynes. He wore his shaggy blond hair in typical seventy's style. The photo captured the twinkle in his soft brown puppy-dog eyes, and highlighted a smile which was a bit too much on the impish side. He had written that his ambition was to "become someone who can help others and bring peace of mind to those who need it." Somehow Melanie didn't think Wyatt had accomplished any of those goals.

His description mentioned he had been heavily involved with sports, reminding Melanie that he had also been heavily involved with a long list of football groupies, none of whom had been her. Until the night of their senior prom, when in typical cliché fashion, she had lost her virginity to him in a sleazy motel room on Route 9. Her only other memory of that night was his promise that he would call her, and how she'd waited two weeks for a phone call that never came.

The last time Melanie had seen Wyatt was at Katie and James' tenth year anniversary party, and although Katie had mentioned that Wyatt had moved back to town and opened some kind of stationery store, there was very little more she wanted to know about him. Melanie closed the book and returned it to the shelf along with the memories of a past life which seemed to belong to someone else. She no longer needed, wanted nor desired anyone or anything from those long ago far away days.

Especially Wyatt Gaynes.

***

This program has performed an illegal operation and will be shut down. If the problem persists, contact the program vendor.

"Darn! I thought DSL would have taken care of this by now," Katie yelled at the computer. While she waited for the re-boot, she opened her year book and began putting colored stickers over the photographs; green for those who had sent in their reservation checks, blue on those who said they were definitely coming, but had not as yet paid, and red on those she hadn't heard from at all. Looking at the small number of green compared to the other two colors, she was beginning to think that her girlfriend was right. Less than half of the class had responded to the committee's invitation and if they didn't get a better response in the next six months, there might not be much of a reunion for them to attend.

High school had never been kind to Katie. She never felt pretty or popular and wasn't very comfortable around people. As a result, she had kept a low profile through most of her high school years. She didn't want to stand out, or become anymore of an oddity then she felt.

She married James O'Brien, the first boy she fell in love with, three months after graduation. Now, the mother of two grown sons, and the wife of a Minnesota State Senator, she finally found the confidence she'd lacked in her youth. Over the years a very determined, strong-willed woman began to replace the shy, insecure teenager whose image was permanently captured in between the yearbook jacket.

Katie looked at the photograph of a girl she only barely recognized. Back then she'd worn her light brown hair short and parted it in the middle like everyone else. Her blue eyes were hidden behind thick black rimmed glasses, but not like everyone else, she had received a perfect score on the SAT. She smiled when she read her ambition was to work for the C.I.A. An ambition which had been inspired by the old sixties television show and the game she and Melanie had played. Katie recalled how they had creating secret dossiers on two of their male classmates, Charles Haussman and Eric Kramer. Two boys neither one of the girls could stand, and the feeling had been mutual. She also remembered how exciting it had been going undercover and creating a entirely new personality, if only for a little while. But children grow up, television shows get canceled, and real life begins, she thought and she really did enjoy her present reality a great deal more than the fantasy life of her childhood.

Katie looked in the mirror and admired the reflection. Like her mother, she started to turn gray at an early age. She decided to let it go natural so her hair was now a soft silver, and it had helped turn her into a striking woman. Marriage, a family and a husband who was a prominent political figure had given her self-confidence a huge boost which was apparent at every fund raiser and social event she hosted.

She was both flattered and surprised when Stuart Janns suggested she chair their thirtieth reunion committee. Except for sharing Honor Society status with him in high school, she didn't think he'd even noticed her. Remembering the terrible experience and lack of cooperation she'd received from the other committee members when she chaired their twentieth, Katie had refused at first, but after discussing the proposal with her husband, he reminded her how much she had enjoyed the experience, even with the headaches. Besides, it was an election year and any good publicity would help his campaign, so she'd sent Stuart an email agreeing to chair the reunion one last time.

Now, looking at the small pile of acceptance cards, she was beginning to think she had made a mistake. In typical politician fashion, James told her not to worry. The reunion was still six months away, and like an election, most people wait to send in their absentee ballots, or simply show up at the polls at the last minute.

Katie wrote the totals in her record book. Well, since it was James' insistence that I chair this thing, she thought, he's going to have to pay for a high speed modem and a printer.

***

This program has performed an illegal operation and will be shut down. If the problem persists, contact the program vendor.

"DAMMIT Joe, I thought you told me you fixed that bug. You had better be sure that no one else noticed."

Wyatt Gaynes' face was bright red as he nearly threw his fist into the computer screen. Shaken by the sudden violent outburst, the younger man began typing as if his life depended on it. If the rumors about his employer were true, he had little doubt that it did.

"I'm sorry, Mr. Gaynes, but this is a common error. I don't think anyone would give it a second thought."

"Not even if every computer from here to Los Angeles has the exact same error at the exact same time?"

Wyatt began pacing the floor. His hand moved the cigarette from his mouth to his side in rhythm with each step.

"I'm not an expert, Mr. Gaynes. I'm only a second year college computer tech student."

Joe started to argue, but the cold glare coming from Wyatt's eyes froze his vocal cords.

Noticing his obvious anxiety, and realizing Joe needed to calm down until he fixed the computer glitch, Wyatt softened his voice.

"I know you are, Joe, but you're also the brightest computer hacker I know and I'm on a deadline. Something as simple as a synchronized error message could put this entire operation in serious jeopardy. And we wouldn't want that, now, would we?"

In spite of his attempt at a gentler tone, the way Wyatt said the word jeopardy made the hairs on the back of Joe's neck stand straight up. He quickly typed a few more keystrokes and the screen returned to normal.

"That should do it, Mr. Gaynes. If that's all for today, I really have to get back to the dorm. If you want my advice, you need to get someone in here who can better understand what you're trying to do."

"I already have him, Joe. You were only his temporary replacement until he came back from a little assignment I sent him on. Take this and forget you were ever here. Understand?"

Wyatt put five one-hundred dollar bills onto the console. Joe grabbed the money without bothering to count it, stuffed the bills into his pants pocket and climbed up the stairs to the exit, three at a time.

As soon as he heard the outside door close, Wyatt pushed a hidden button under the console and a wooden panel slid open behind him, revealing a computer nerd's idea of heaven. A world map with over five hundred tiny lights lit in red, green and yellow covered the entire back wall. The red LEDs were placed on the cities where Wyatt's plan was already underway, the green ones signified the locations of his contacts, and the yellow were future sites yet to be established.

Wyatt pulled five green lights from the board and replaced them with red ones, then he replaced all but three of the yellow with green. Things were going well, he thought, but not fast enough. Wyatt had a plan and although he was right on schedule, he needed help to complete the final preparations. He was an intelligent man, and an intelligent man knew his limitations. Joe was right; Wyatt did need experts on his team and friends he could rely on. Especially friends with weaknesses he could exploit to his own advantage. He was almost amazed at how easy it had been to manipulate those very friends who were now fully entrenched in his organization. It had only taken a little charm and some cold hard cash to convince them, and he had plenty of both.

Wyatt's plans were set to take place during the weekend of their thirtieth high school reunion. All the players would be in place and he could hardly wait another six months. Wyatt hit a switch and pages of his old yearbook appeared on the wall. The faces of familiar friends filled the screen and from somewhere deep within Wyatt's youth, flashes of warm memories emerged. Katie Conner, he recalled how he hated him calling her K.C., yet she had written that as her nickname next to her graduation photo. Seeing those initials brought an uncharacteristic smile to his face. He looked at the photos of Charles Haussman and Eric Kramer, two boys who had no idea back then how important they would become to him in the present.

Wyatt paused for a moment when an all-too familiar photo of someone he hadn't seen for nearly twenty years filled the screen. He stared at the photo of Melanie Tyler a lot longer than he had the others, finally forcing himself to turn the page to the athletic teams section. He stared at his sports photos with disdain. Along side his name were the captions; second string quarterback, second place wrestler, second string basketball squad. And the nickname title Mr. Silver that was printed under his photo and labeled him for all eternity.

Well, he'd show them, he thought. By the time their reunion was over, no one in Abbeyville, or anywhere else in the world was ever going to refer to him as Mr. Silver again.

After nearly thirty years, he was back in the game and this time no one, not even his big brother, was going to stop him from taking home the gold.

***

This program has performed an illegal operation and will be shut down. If the problem persists, contact the program vendor.
In an underground conference room located a few miles from Wyatt's operation, two men read what appeared

to be a common computer error message, but as soon as it came on the screen, lights and buzzers blared a warning that put several systems on high alert.

"Don, did you see that?" Stuart Janns said to his partner.

"Yes. That bug originated right here in Abbeyville."

"Seems like Wyatt's computer system isn't as secure as he thinks it is."

"For now you're right, Stu, but he still has six months before your reunion to get it operational," Don said. "We should have our operatives in place well before he has a chance to debug his system, but just in case something goes wrong, how is plan B coming?"

"See for yourself," Stuart turned off the lights and two photos appeared on the screen. "It took a little arm-twisting, but they'll both be positioned exactly where we'll need them when the time comes."

"They look perfect, especially the one on the right," Don said, pointed to the yearbook pictures of a bobbed haired, horned- rimmed-glasses wearing Katie Connor O'Brien. On the right, wearing bell bottoms, tie-dyed t-shirt and holding up a two-fingered peace sign was one rebellious protestor named Melanie Tyler.

Chapter Two
Class of '72 High School Reunion
Friday Night Cocktail Party

The Grand Ballroom of the Abbeyville Hilton was designed to accommodate more than five hundred, but for this event only a hundred and seventy-five invitees and guests had confirmed reservations. Katie had worked tirelessly for over a year planning the reunion, but she was beginning to think the entire weekend was going to be a disaster.

Abbeyville High School boasted a graduating class of one-hundred-thirty-seven, which was quite large in a town of only five thousand residents. Unlike the majority of her classmates who had gone off to attend out-of-state colleges and moved on to live in various parts of the world, Katie had attended Minnesota State and had stayed in her hometown to raise her family with her husband James.

James O'Brien obtained his law degree, past the bar and was hired by a small law firm the year their first son was born. Two years and another son later, James opened his own office specializing in environmental law and representing low-income farmers through the Minnesota Family Farm Law Project.

With Katie arranging his social calendar and business engagements, James grew his practice into one of the largest in the county. Although his work took him away from his family for extended periods, Katie was content to be the typical stay at home mom, raising their two sons and volunteering at local charity events.

It wasn't long before members of the Chamber of Commerce approached James to run for a seat on the City Council, where his warm personality and honest reputation helped him win the mayor's race a few years later. He continued to ride his rising political star all the way to the capitol, eventually being elected the youngest member of the Minnesota Senate. Yet, even with his ability to fill an auditorium during a political debate, even he wasn't enough of a draw to entice his own classmates to attend another reunion.

Katie was looking forward to the celebration and was devastated by the lack of enthusiasm she had received, not only from her classmates, but from those who had helped her organize the two prior events. When she had started looking for additional help from the twentieth reunion committee, she'd found that most of them had moved out of town, or had lost interest.

When Stuart called with the dire prediction that if she didn't chair the committee for the thirtieth, there probably wouldn't be a reunion at all, she reluctantly agreed, even though she knew she would have a great deal to do bring it together. Fortunately there were enough funds remaining in the reunion account for the deposit on the ballroom and food, but not much left for a band or decorations.

Her "save the date" e-mail announcements were met with more polite declines than acceptances and when even her best friend told her that she might not be able to make it, Katie was nearly ready to call it quits.

Ever the supportive husband, James offered his assistance by asking his staff to volunteer to help. He used his political charm on several of his business contacts who contributed exciting door prizes to the event. A local printer donated the invitations, and soon after they were mailed, the acceptances began arriving with more positive responses. Katie began to relax, but she could feel her anxiety level increase as Friday night's opening weekend cocktail party was about to begin.

Katie would never admit to anyone, especially her husband, how desperately she wanted the weekend to be a success. Katie knew her classmates only thought of her as a shy air-head whose only real accomplishment had been winning a red ribbon at the Minnesota State Fair for her blueberry pie. No one except Melanie and James knew that Katie had graduated Summa Cum Laude or that her I.Q. was rated above 165.

Their twentieth reunion had been a huge disappointment. Personalities had been altered by divorce, death and distance. The attendees treated her almost as badly as they had in high school. Almost no one had recognized her, and those that did were not at all diplomatic in their harsh criticisms and negative comments on her appearance. She didn't expect anything to have changed much in ten years.

Looking at all of the empty chairs, Katie's spirits were beginning to deflate as quickly as the last helium-filled balloon rose to the ceiling. She was beginning to wonder if even those who had confirmed their reservation would bother showing. They had already lost several classmates to unfortunate deaths, and the big five-o was just around the corner. Emphasizing that it could be the last chance they might ever have to see their friends and former classmates, and citing the long list of gifts her husband's staff had provided for the attendees, Katie convinced many of her classmates that they just could not miss the one reunion she had worked so hard to organize.

Fortunately, her persuasive technique had worked, even with those who still lived in town and had never attended previous reunions. Katie had even managed to contact a few retired teachers, who were thrilled to have been invited and they all promised to attend. It was a good sign, Katie thought, but while the verbal acceptances had been easy, the actual checks were taking a lot longer to arrive.

Katie walked through the partition door to the adjacent room where the cocktail party was going to be held later that evening. She meticulously matched yearbook photos to name tags, and placed them alongside the guest book on the registration table at the entrance. On the left side of the room the bartender was setting up the wine and beer bar. On the right, the staff was preparing the plates for the hors d'oeuvres. On the center stage, the band was checking the sound system. Directly above them, in huge letters of blue and gold hung a huge banner that read; Welcome Class of 1972.

With the room beginning to look more festive, Katie started to feel a bit more confident.As she was heading to the lobby, her cell phone began ringing. The caller ID told her immediately who it was.

"Melanie!" She exclaimed, "Where are you?"

"Surprise, I'm made it!"

Even though Katie has suspected her girlfriend was going to attend, she was relieved and excited that her suspicions proved to be correct.

"I took the red-eye and checked-in a little while ago," Melanie said. "I was going to call you when I landed, but I couldn't get a signal until just now, and this is a brand new phone."

"I'm so happy to hear your voice, even with the bad reception that's not unusual for this part of the state," Katie said. "James has been trying to push for a new cell tower, but he's not getting much support."

"Well, it seems to be working fine now. Where are you?"

"I'm in the lobby, c'mon down. I was just leaving to head home, but I'll wait for you."

Several minutes later, the elevator door opened and the two women greeted each other like they were back in high school. They hugged, they screamed, and jumped around like teenagers. The other hotel guests were staring, but the girls didn't care.

"Has it really been twenty years?" Katie said, "Mel, you don't look a day older than thirty."

"Thanks, Katie. You can thank my hair stylist Sophia for that. She's a genius!"

Melanie glanced at her reflection in the hall mirror. Even though she had flown for three-and-a-half-hours to Duluth, then driven two more hours to the one and only five star hotel in Abbeyville, she looked wide awake. She was dressed in a revealing cotton sundress, not the usual Minnesotan attire, and was getting a few less than approving stares from the women guests and even some staff.

"I guess I should have worn something a bit more modest, but it was so damn hot when I got off that plane. I've forgotten how humid this part of the country is in the summer."

"Well, just as long as you don't stay outside too long without wearing jeans and a long sleeve shirt. Our mosquitoes love imported blood, don't cha' know. I can't believe you're really here, or that you kept it a secret for all these months."

"Yes, I'm good at keeping secrets, don't cha know," Melanie imitated Katie's Minnesotan twang, with a hint of a tease. "Actually, it was Stuart who convinced me to come, so you owe him one."

"Yeah, well he also convinced me to chair this thing, so I think we're even. Do you know if anyone else from our class has checked in yet?"

The sentence was more of an optimistic statement than a question.

"Not so far, but I did arrive early and went directly to my room for a quick shower. It took me awhile to find this place. The last time I was in Abbeyville, I stayed at the Best Western."

"Well, once Jack Gaynes became CEO of the paper mill, he needed a first-class hotel for his business clients, so he convinced the Hilton chain to come to our little town."

"I bet that went over well with his brother," Melanie said, nonchalantly.

"Not nearly as badly as when Jack married Wyatt's girlfriend," Katie replied. "Don't ya just love small town gossip?"

So, Jack married Brenda, interesting. Melanie thought. She immediately changed the subject.

"I'm sure people will start arriving later, since the cocktail party starts at eight, and the main event isn't until tomorrow night."

"I hope you're right," Katie said, "Meanwhile, we have plenty of time to catch up during the cocktail party. James promised to be home from St. Paul before it started so he'd have time to change, but it might be late. The legislature called a special session this morning to vote on some kind of toxic chemical bill before the summer recess. As usual, our state legislature has perfect timing."

"You go on home and get ready. I'll stake out a seat at the bar and let you know who else arrives."

"Still playing spies, Mel?" Katie laughed. "Well at least now we have cell phones so we won't need to pass coded notes. I'll be back in a couple of hours."

Katie left the hotel and Melanie took a seat at the lobby bar from where she had a clear view of the entrance and the elevator, but no one could see her. Like old times, she thought. Abbeyville was such a small, boring town, she almost wished she were a spy on an undercover mission.

"I've been living in fantasyland for too many years," She accidently said aloud.

"I don't know," a man's voice responded. "I kind of like living in a small boring town. It's better on the heart."

It took Melanie a moment to recover her embarrassment when she realized the bartender had overhead what she had said. She found herself feeling a bit self-conscious when she noticed his amused smile that was attached to an usually attractive face. Unusual for Abbeyville, Minnesota, she thought.

"I'm sorry, I didn't mean for anyone to hear that. I'll have a glass of white wine, please...Don," she read his name tag.

He smiled politely and poured her order.

"Thanks. Not to be trite, but you don't look like you're the small town Midwestern type."

Melanie took a sip of her drink feeling the wine warm her cheeks or maybe it was the heat being generated by Don's gaze.

Don busied himself wiping off the counter trying not to think that Melanie's photos didn't even come close to how she looked in person.

"No? And what does a small town Midwestern type look like?"

"You know extra fat around the middle to protect from the winter cold for one."

She pointed to Don's abdomen.

"Well, it is summer, don't cha know. But you're right. I only moved here a few years ago. I think I put on a few pounds, but it's not that bad."

Don patted his abdomen, pointing out to Melanie who didn't need the gesture to notice that he didn't have an ounce of flab.

"You waiting for someone?" Don asked.

"No, why?"

"I just noticed you keep staring at the entrance."

"Oh, that. I'm sort of spying for my girlfriend. It's our thirtieth high school reunion weekend and she's nervous that no one will show up."

Melanie tried to keep her eyes on the door, but the view in front of her was a lot more interesting. Don was most definitely not from Abbeyville, no one with such deep blue eyes and strong muscular physique could live in a town where the most excitement came from hanging out at the local bar watching the Viking's lose another SuperBowl.

"You don't look old enough for this to be your thirtieth reunion," Don said with a grin.

"See, now I know you're not from around here. Our bartenders don't know how to compliment a woman, unless they want to get a bigger tip."

"And how do you know that wasn't my intention?"

"I think you have way too much class for false flattery, or ulterior motives. I'm from Los Angeles, and I can size up the type in about ten seconds and I've been here..." Melanie checked her watch, "fifteen minutes."

"And you're almost finished with that glass of wine. Want another?"

Melanie was going to decline, until she saw two very familiar figures enter the hotel. "Absolutely. Make it a double."

"Ah, I take it you recognized a few old friends."

"I wouldn't call them friends, exactly. That's Charles Haussman and Eric Kramer. I was hoping they wouldn't be here, but I'm sure Katie will be happy. Excuse me a second, I have to make a call."

"Sure."

Don refilled her glass then turned his back and pretended to write up Melanie's tab. He made sure she didn't notice that he was talking into a fountain pen.

"Stu," he whispered. "Haussman and Kramer just arrived. No, I don't see Gaynes, but I'll let ya know if he shows. I just met Melanie Tyler. You were certainly right about her. Gotta go."

Don put the pen back into his shirt pocket just as Melanie returned to her seat. She took a large sip of her drink, never taking her eyes off of the two men who were carrying on what seemed to be a very heated conversation.

"So, was your other spy happy with your report?" Don asked.

"Spy? Oh, you mean Katie. I'd say it was mixed. She was glad that there were people starting to arrive, but not so much that those two had arrived first. As you can imagine in a small town everyone has a bit of a past, and her and I go way back with those two."

"Old boyfriends?"

"Hardly. More like old adversaries. It's funny that you should mention spying. When Katie and I were in Junior High, we went on a little mission and really got even with those two. Even now, seeing them together makes my skin crawl."

"Well, before this place gets too busy, do you want to tell me about it. I'm a good listener, being a bartender and all."

"And a bartender never repeats anything he hears, right?"

Melanie wasn't sure she wanted to tell Don about her and Katie's dark secret, but there was something in his eyes that made her feel that she could tell him just about anything.

"Fill this up again."

She pointed to her empty wine glass.

"And I'll fill you in on all the details. But I have to warn you, if you reveal to anyone what I'm about to tell you, I'll have to kill you." Melanie smiled.

Don made a zipper motion across his lips and held up his right palm. "I swear no one will ever get me to talk."

And they certainly have tried, Don thought.

"Well, it all started the weekend of our Junior High Valentine's dance," Melanie began. "Katie and I were getting off the bus on our way to class..."

Chapter Three
1967

On a typically frigid February morning, thirteen- year-old Melanie Tyler exited the warmth of the heated school bus and rushed through the heavy insulated glass doorway which led into the Junior High section of Abbeyville Public School. She headed to her locker and met her best friend, who was brushing snow from her coat.

"Katie, what happened?" She asked.

"Eric and Chuck threw snowballs at me again. That's the third time this week. They nearly broke my glasses and my mom can't afford to buy another pair." Katie was close to tears.

Melanie helped her friend clean off the remaining snow before removing her own coat and boots. As she opened her locker, a flurry of red paper hearts flew onto the floor, each one with the same stick-figure picture of a girl with huge frizzy hair and exaggerated breasts. Happy Valentine's Day, loser, was scrawled over the face. Melanie angrily crumpled them before tossing them into the trash.

"You would think those jerks would have better things to do," Melanie said. "My mom said the reason they tease us is because they like us."

"Yeah, my mom says the same thing. I can't imagine what they might do if they actually hated us," Katie replied. "We'd better get to class, the bell is going to ring in about ten seconds. Don't forget the notebook."

"I don't let this out of my sight."

Melanie slid a small black spiral book in between her English and Biology textbooks. She followed her friend into their first period class, purposefully avoiding looking at their two nemeses who were laughing and whispering with several other boys in the back of the room. She took her assigned seat next to Katie who was giving the boys a fierce drop dead look.

After attendance was taken and the Pledge of Allegiance recited, the first of seven period classes began, but Melanie wasn't paying attention to the grammar lesson. Even though she appeared to be taking notes, she was, in fact, writing to Katie using a secret code they had created so they could communicate with each other without anyone being able to know what they were saying.

The girls had created their private communication code the previous winter, after Eric had intercepted a note she had passed to Katie telling her about a crush she had on the second-string quarterback on the Junior Varsity football team. Eric had grabbed the note from Katie's hand and showed it to Chuck. Then, the two of them had read it aloud, just as the entire junior high football team, and their entourage of cheerleaders, past them in the hallway on their way to practice.

Everyone had laughed at her, especially the head cheerleader who was walking arm in arm with that very same quarterback. Of course the boy had also been embarrassed, so much so, that he'd totally stopped speaking to her, even after school, and his cheerleader girlfriend had made it clear that Melanie had better stay away from her boyfriend.

Melanie never forgot how betrayed she had felt that day, and not even Katie's offer to go ice-skating on the lake had been able to cheer her. She cried the entire bus ride home, where, after watching their favorite spy program, she created the special alphabet code which she taught it to Katie the following day.

A few weeks later, the girls purposely left a coded note on the floor by her locker. They hid behind a wall and watched as Eric picked up the paper and showed it to Chuck. Melanie was very pleased when she saw the look of frustration on their faces when they tried to read it, and failed. She felt satisfied that the boys would never have another opportunity to embarrass them by reading private notes again, but the teasing only became more irritating and frequent. Even though the girl's parents had spoken to the principal, the boy's families were so well connected with the school board that, other than a firm reprimand, no punishment was ever dispensed.

After the snow ball assault on Katie and those nasty valentines cascading from her locker, Melanie was more determined than ever that she and Katie needed to come up with a more drastic plan that would put an end to their enemy's harassment once and for all.

When the teacher turned her back to write the assignment on the blackboard, Melanie handed Katie the coded note, which simply confirmed their weekly plan to meet at her house to watch the latest episode of their favorite television show. They had watched every Affair since the very first airing on September 22, 1964, and were such fans, they created their own spy headquarters in the basement of Melanie's house.

During the Cuban Missile Crises in 1962, Melanie's father, like so many families in small towns across America, had built a bomb shelter in the basement of their home. What had once served as a safe haven for nature's occasional tornado, had been transformed into a fortress against a potential manmade disaster. Since Abbeyville was less than 150 miles from Duluth everyone in the small community feared the possibility of radiation fallout. Seeing the concrete blocks in her basement had so upset Melanie's mother that after the crises was over, she had insisted that they conceal the concrete walls, so they had it covered over with wooden paneling and turned the basement into a rec room, complete with a full service bar. The door to the shelter itself was hidden behind a removable panel making the entrance appear almost invisible to anyone who didn't know it existed.

It was the perfect location for two young girls to create a private place away from their parents, where they could tell secrets and gossip about boys. After the premier of The Man from UNCLE, the Tyler's bomb shelter was transformed into Melanie and Katie's very own spy headquarters.

The girls equipped the room with a cardboard filing cabinet and hung a blackboard and posters of the shows two male stars. Melanie's mother's Lazy Susan serving tray resembled the revolving work table on the show and of course they had the full collection of every merchandise tie-in from toy guns to the board game.

While in their secret room, Katie and Melanie had privately joked that Eric and Chuck could have been members of the evil organization THRUSH, and after the note incident, they began to accumulate files and plot a way to get even, but there was never enough real evidence to show their parents or the school authorities. Without any real proof, the girls knew they would be accused of having overactive imaginations and their parents would just say being teased by thirteen-year-old boys was just part of growing up in a small town. But the girls were determined.

The day of the snowball incident, Melanie and Katie were sitting on the bench during girls' basketball waiting for their names to be called. Although they each enjoyed playing sports, neither girl was particularly athletic, so the all-girl gym class was more a time to chat without any boys around to distract them.

"You know, it really is too bad there isn't a real secret spy organization to fight the bad guys and win every week," Katie said to Melanie. "We could sure use their help with Eric and Chuck."

"Well, maybe we'll get an idea after tonight's show. I'm not about to start throwing snowballs, but we really need to do something. Can you think of anyone else who they've been annoying who would want to join us?" Melanie said.

"Hey, what about asking Wyatt to help? I think he might like to play spy with us. He wasn't all that happy with Chuck and Eric after they read your note last year. They really embarrassed him."

"Embarrassed him?" Melanie said. "Are you kidding? Wyatt hasn't spoken to me since. He still blames me for his break up with Janet, if you can believe that. You should ask James, I think he likes you."

Melanie didn't tell her friend that James had told her that he wanted to ask Katie to the Valentines dance, and Melanie had told him that he should because she thought Katie liked him, too.

"I think you're trying to play matchmaker, but that's a great idea. He is kinda cute and they're in the same math class. James doesn't like them very much either. He might be able to find out something, even though I know he's going to be busy studying for midterms next week."

"We really need to get these guys soon, so we can both concentrate on studying," Melanie said. "Tonight's basketball game was cancelled and our Drama Club rehearsal had to be moved to tomorrow afternoon. When you see James at lunch, invite him to come over to my place tonight. You can make an excuse that we want to study together."

"Well, I hate to lie, but if you really think James likes me, then I'll do it." Katie replied, trying unsuccessfully not to blush.

The gym teacher blew the whistle and Melanie ran onto the court, but her mind wasn't on basketball. James was a nice boy, which would mean that Eric and Chuck would never suspect him of helping them, but she really didn't want to get him in trouble if he were to be discovered.

As they had planned, Katie sat next to James during lunch while Melanie joined the table with the students of the Drama Club who were discussing their next production.

Melanie's attention was split between their conversation regarding the French farce, Thieves Carnival, and the interaction between James and Katie. There was no doubt in her mind that James was accepting her invitation to study, and Katie was agreeing to attend the dance with James.

Melanie's suspicions were confirmed when Katie told her James had accepted her invitation and would be by Melanie's house after supper. The girls managed to avoid Eric and Chuck for the rest of the day since the boys' last class was gym and there was always a practice, even when no game was scheduled.

James arrived at Melanie's several minutes after Katie, greeted Melanie's parents, then followed the girls down the stairs leading to the basement. Believing they were going to study, James sat down at the center table and opened his books. He was a bit shaken when Katie closed the books, took his hand, and led him into the secret room behind the panel.

"Wow, Mel!" James exclaimed once his eyes adjusted to the semi-darkness, "This is super neat!"

"We know, but before we show you anything more, you have to take an oath and swear not to tell anyone." Melanie said. "Raise your right hand and repeat after me." Katie added.

James moved his hand as instructed and echoed Katie and Melanie's words.

"I swear to never tell anyone, not my family, or my parents, or my friends, anything about this room, or what we talk about. Cross my heart and hope to die," Melanie and Katie said in unison, crossing their hearts.

"Cross my heart and hope to die." James mimicked the gesture as he repeated the last phrase.

"Ok, now we can tell you why you're here."

The girls spent the next half hour giving James a brief explanation about the room, their problems with Chuck and

Eric, and why they had invited him to share their secret. Melanie opened the top cabinet and removed the files that had the names Eric Kramer and Charles Haussman written on the front, and showed them to James.

"Look through these files and see if you can come up with something."

James scanned through the pages, then closed the files and said, "I think I may have what you two need, but it's not in these files and I don't have any real proof."

Melanie picked up a notebook and waited for James to continue.

"We'll worry about proof later," she said. "Tell us what you've got on those creeps!"

"After practice today, I saw Eric and Chuck talking with Wyatt kinda secret like. I thought they were discussing the game plan, but then I saw Eric and Chuck give Wyatt a stack of bills and Wyatt handed then some papers. I can't be certain, but they were acting really strange when I walked by, but I could see them in the mirror. They were putting the papers into their gym lockers."

"James, that's great!" Melanie said, giving James a kiss on the cheek.

"You're the best!" Katie started to repeat Melanie's thank you kiss when he moved his head so her lips connected with his, and the kiss lasted a bit longer than Melanie's.

"Hey you guys. This is our spy headquarters, not your personal love den!" Melanie kidded.

Katie moved back into her chair.

"Mel, you said you had rehearsal tomorrow. Do you think you could take James and me with you, so we can check out the locker?"

"You bet, Katie! Now, let's get out of here and watch the real fake spies on TV."

Saturday afternoon Melanie left the auditorium during a scene where her character wasn't on stage. She ran down the hall and unlocked the outside door which led to the gym and let in James and Katie. Knowing that they only had a few minutes, they headed to the boy's locker room. James entered first to be certain the room was empty, then motioned for the girls to follow.

Each locker was tagged with the name of the owner, lined up alphabetically, so it didn't take Katie long to find the one belonging to Eric. The locks were so old, it only took a slight pull for her to release the latch. The girls held their breath when the stench of dirty socks and sneaker escaped into their nostrils, but it was only for a second as Katie found the papers she was looking for.

They both had to stifle their cries of excitement when they saw what Katie was holding; a completed answer bluebook for the upcoming math midterm exam, and on the front cover, written in his own handwriting, was the name Eric Kramer.

Katie opened Chuck's locker and found another answer bluebook with his name on it. Melanie checked the time and seeing she needed to be back on stage in five minutes, closed the lockers and quietly left the gym, the test papers hidden securely in Katie's purse.

"I can't believe we did that!" Melanie whispered.

"What do we do now? Should we show the principal?" Katie replied.

"We'll figure it out tonight at my place. I have to get back on stage. I'll call you when I get home and we can make our plans later tonight. James, you go home, too."

"Ok, I'll see you later. Good luck girls, and Katie, please be careful."

"Don't worry, James. We'll let you know how it goes and thanks for the help." Katie said.

"Always happy to help out an UNCLE agent," James smiled and waved good-bye to the two girls as he headed home.

That night, Katie and Melanie finalized their plan to deal with Eric and Charles once and for all. They realized that if they reported them to the principal, or the math teacher, that they would not only have to reveal the name of the student who had told them about the cheating, but also who else was involved, and admit they had broken into the boy's locker room. They both knew that although it might have been the right thing to do in their parent's point of view, they were certain the rest of their classmates wouldn't think so. They had just started Junior High and being labeled a tattletale was not the reputation either of them wished to be tagged with for the next five years of public school.

After reading through several notes they had taken from watching past episodes of the television show, they came up with a plan. Melanie went upstairs and asked her father to borrow his Polaroid and his newspaper. She brought them back to Katie and took two photos of Katie holding the covers of the answer booklets, alongside the headline of the daily paper, then put the answer books into their filing cabinet.

Early Monday morning, Melanie put the photos into an envelope and placed one in Eric's locker and one in Chuck's, along with a note which read. Meet us after school by the football bleachers, or else.

Eric didn't say much when they arrived at the bleachers, but Chuck wasn't about to let them win without putting up a fight.

"These aren't ours," he lied. "I don't know what you girls are trying to do, but making up some fake pictures isn't going to work."

"Shut up, Chuck," Eric whispered, "As far as I'm concerned, it's working fine."

"We know you bought the test answers from Wyatt." Katie said. "And you know these are real because we found them in your lockers. Don't try to throw them out, we have copies hidden in a very secure place."

"Who told you?" Eric's freckles more pronounced since most of the blood had nearly drained from his face.

"None of your business. Let's just say it was a reliable source. But don't worry, we're not going to tell anyone," Melanie said. The boys started to relax a bit, and she continued, "As long as you agree to our demands."

"Whatever you girls want." Eric's voice was starting to crack.

"Shut up, Eric and let them talk," Chuck shouted, still not wanting to admit defeat.

"No more throwing snowballs, or putting things in our locker for starters," Katie began.

"And any other teasing of any kind will stop," Melanie continued. "And you won't tell anyone, not even Wyatt...especially Wyatt, that we found out about the cheating."

"Don't talk to us, don't talk about us, just pretend we don't exist and we'll do the same. Got it?"

Katie gave them a stern look that made it obvious to both boys that they had met their match.

The boys reluctantly agreed to the girls' demands and Katie tore up the photographs, but as promised, Melanie kept copies in her basement files just to make sure the boys wouldn't go back on their word.

Eric and Charles both failed the midterm and had to spend their summer vacation re-taking seventh grade math. Katie and James were inseparable and by the end of Junior High, had put the incident behind them. Melanie's performance in the play received great reviews, and she went on to star in many more productions throughout their high school years. True to her word, she never told anyone about the math midterm, or what she and Katie had done to Eric and Charles. Until now.

"The television series ended the following year and my mom turned our basement U.N.C.L.E headquarters into a much more friendly storage room for her canned jams and jellies," Melanie told Don. "But I have to say, I was really glad that the Man from UNCLE gave us the courage to stand up to the two bullies."

"Glad to hear it. Did that other boy ever fess up to stealing the test in the first place?" Don asked.

"Wyatt you mean? No. But he did apologize to me at the Valentines dance for what Charles and Eric had done with that note. He said at the time he was just being a jerk to impress the guys and whoever he was dating at the time. We sort of began seeing each other in secret, he didn't think his jock buddies would approve of him dating an acting geek, at least that's what he told me. He came to nearly all of my performances and I'd sneak him into that room in the basement after the final curtain call. My parents never found out."

"It sounds like you would have made a really good spy," Don grinned.

"I seriously doubt that. Spies aren't usually as trusting as I was back then. Speak of past mistakes, see that guy over there?"

Melanie motioned to an overly animated figure dressed in beige shorts and a flashy Floridian print short-sleeve shirt. From where she was sitting, Melanie couldn't tell if his tan was natural, or sprayed on. She could have said the same about his sandy blond hair, which he kept pushing from his forehead with his fingers. It was a purposeful gesture indicating to the balding person he was talking to that he had retained part of his youth that the other man had obviously lost.

A sudden chill came over Melanie and she shivered slightly. She wasn't sure if it was the temperature in the lobby, or the memory of her youthful indiscretions that had caused the reaction.

"The one who looked like he just stepped off a cruise ship?"

Don nodded in the direction where Melanie was looking.

"Yeah, that's Wyatt Gaynes. Remember I told you he would come to my place after the performances? Nothing physical ever happened. All we ever did was talk. We had some really deep conversations about books and movies and even politics. Then the next day at school he would act as if he didn't even know me. When I told him I had been accepted to U.C.L.A. I thought he'd be excited for me. Instead, he became very angry. Even though I promised we would see each other when I came home on vacations, that wasn't good enough for Wyatt. I guess he thought I was going to stay here with him, if you can believe that. I'd never seen him that mad, and if I hadn't already bought my prom dress, I never would have gone with him."

"Did you at least have a good time?" Don asked.

"Yes, I suppose. That night he was back to his charming self. The guy was like two different people and unfortunately, I fell for the one who I thought was sincere."

Don could almost feel the invisible connection that evidently still existed between the woman with the story and the man she couldn't seem to take her eyes from.

"And I assume he wasn't?" he asked.

"The lying creep dumped me right after senior prom."

"Oh, I see."

Don had a feeling that a lot more happened after senior prom than Melanie was willing to share with a stranger, not even one with a bottle of wine in his hand.

"Need a refill?" he tried a weak grin.

Melanie returned his smile, but refused the drink. "No thanks, I see more of our class coming in and I need to get changed for the cocktail party. If you happen to serve any other members of my class, I trust you'll honor the bartender-drinker confidentiality and not say anything about what I told you."

"What exactly did you tell me?"

Don gave Mel a little wink.

"Thanks. So glad I didn't bore you with my little trip down memory lane."

"Not at all. I found that story of your small town history quite interesting. See you later."

Quite interesting, he thought as he watched Melanie walk toward the elevator. Stu was right when he suggested recruiting her and Katie for the mission. At first he didn't think the women would want to work with them because of classmate loyalties, but after he heard Melanie's story he was convinced they not only could help, but would be more than willing to bring Haussman, Kramer, and especially Gaynes to justice. And much to his amazement, he found himself looking forward to working with the very fascinating Melanie Tyler a lot more than he had originally thought.

For now Don had to put all thoughts about the mission, and Melanie, on hold as the reunion crowd began to fill the bar stools, and they were a very thirsty crowd.

Chapter Four

The Abbeyville Hilton suite provided the luxury of a relaxing hot tub, which Melanie took full advantage of before getting ready for the cocktail party. She unpacked her belongings, hung the black and white designer dress she was planning on wearing to the banquet the following night, and did her best to iron away the travel wrinkles from the ocean blue sleeveless dress she would be wearing to meet her former classmates whom she hadn't seen since they received their diplomas.

Melanie was a bit surprised by her reaction when she'd told Don about her former high school crush. She hadn't seen Wyatt Gaynes in nearly twenty years, but it seemed to her that the old adage was true; no matter how many candles you blow out each year, some flames continue to burn.

Melanie pushed the then and gone from her mind and continued to apply her make-up to the face in the here and now. She wished she had changed her attire before she met the bartender, but he hadn't seemed to have noticed. She certainly wasn't in the habit of talking about her personal life to complete strangers, but since she was only going to be in town for a few days, she really hadn't minded. She wasn't sure if she was looking forward to seeing old friends she hadn't seen in thirty years, or one very interesting stranger she had just met an hour ago.

After giving herself a final visual inspection in the full length mirror Melanie proceeded to the elevator which would transport her thirty years into the past. She pressed the down button just as a few other guests approached the doors.

"Melanie Tyler, is that you? A familiar male's voice asked.

"Bobbie! Bobbie Johnson? Yes, it's me. I thought you were in Europe."

"No, my company moved to Florida about six years ago. This is my wife, Christine."

They continued to engage in small talk as the elevator stopped at each floor and more members of the class of '72 entered and exchanged greetings all the way down to the lobby floor. Melanie glanced at the bar briefly to see if Don was there, but the crowd blocked her view, so she continued walking to the reception area.

Katie was seated at the registration table, taking checks and handing out name badges which had the yearbook photo on each one, so that everyone would know who they had been in their youth. The married women's name tags had both their married and maiden names written on them.

"Is James here?" Melanie put on her name tag.

"No. I guess he's still at the capital. I'm sure he'll be here soon. Go on inside and I'll be there as soon as everyone else arrives.

Melanie walked into the banquet room where there was a smaller bar set up with wine and beer.

Melanie did a quick 360 of the room. Katie really didn't have anything to worry about, she thought. Nearly every chair was occupied by a familiar body or the date of a familiar body. Melanie noticed just how much had not changed in three decades. The popular clique was huddled together in the back of the room exchanging photos of children and grandchildren and dishing dirt on the other attendees. It was painfully obvious to everyone else but them that they had let their beauty regimens go once they landed a husband.

The nerds were still nerds, only with cell phones instead of calculators. The former sports jocks were giving high-fives to their former glory days, while ignoring the fact they had gained as much weight around their waists as they had lost hair on their heads. She walked out to the patio to have one of her three-a-week allotted cigarettes, and was very relieved to see some of the members of her old drama club enjoying the same.

"Jennifer. Caroline. Francis. Hank. So this is where the cool kids are hiding."

She greeted her old friends as if she'd just seen them last week.

"Well, look who finally decided to attend a reunion," Jennifer said. "Ok, I win. Everybody pay up.""Oh, c'mon Jennifer. You actually made a bet on me? Didn't you see my name tag on the table?"

"Yes, like we saw it at the fifth, tenth and twentieth reunion," Hank said. "I thought it was a sure thing you'd be a no-show again this year, but it appears not." He opened his wallet and reluctantly handed Jennifer the money. "So, how's the big Hollywood star?" he teased.

Damn her contract, Melanie thought. These were the people who had given birth to her acting career. They had spent long hours, and nearly every weekend in rehearsals, performing plays for the community. If she couldn't trust her fellow thespians, who could she trust? She gave the answer in the well-known voice of Maggie Franklin, using a line from their ninth grade production of Thieves Carnival:

"Nothing to do, no where to go, and all the men are hideous. Quite, quite hideous." She took a drag from the cigarette, smiled and waited for their reaction.

"Hey, Mel, that's very good," Francis said.

"Yeah, you sound just like the character from that cartoon show, what's her name, Maggie something or other?" Jennifer added, "Quit kidding around Mel. Tell us what you've really been doing these past thirty years."

Melanie tried another line using a different voice, that of the female dinosaur from the latest full-length animated feature, but apparently none of her friends had seen the movie. Well, Melanie thought, I guess my secret is safe. She gave her next response was in her normal voice.

"I've been doing some extra work and a few small plays," She said, before changing the subject. "I don't see Debra or Cindy, are they here?

"Well, Cindy left the theater to become a lawyer. The last we heard, she'd left that too, got married and had a few kids. We haven't seen her in years." Francis said.

"Debra studied classical piano at Julliard and became a concert pianist. At the twentieth, she told us she recorded a few CDs, but her husband was getting tired of her frequent trips away from home, so she gave up her career and now only performs locally. I doubt she'll be here, I think she's too embarrassed."

"I would be too, Jennifer, if I had to give up my dream for some man," Caroline said, "I'm totally happy right here in Abbeyville, teaching drama to the next generation of wannabee actors."

"Speaking of wannabees, did you see who just walked by?"

Hank didn't even try to hide his disgust.

"Mr. Silver himself. Rumor has it that he never got over his father making big brother Jack the CEO of the papermill, but you'd never know it by the way he's stuttin' his stuff. I once made the mistake of asking him for a job at his little print shop after Jack moved the company headquarters to Mankato and a bunch of us were laid off. The bastard just laughed in my face. Then, he turns around and hires Chuck, of all people. Can you believe that? Told me he had some sense of loyalty because they played on the football team together. If you want my opinion, I think Wyatt is the biggest actor of all of us."

"He's definitely got the bullshit down, that's for sure. Oh crap, he's coming over," Jennifer said. "I'm going to the ladies room, Mel, you want to join us?"

The three women rose to leave, but Melanie's legs refused to follow.

"That's Ok. I'm fine," she said.

In reality she was anything but fine. It had been twenty years since she'd last seen Wyatt, but ever since she'd seen him in the lobby, she could not stop thinking about what she was going to say if and when he approached her. Try as she could to avoid looking at him, she found herself nearly staring.

Melanie finished the rest of her drink in one gulp and started coughing immediately. Hank began patting her on the back, which made her cough even louder, and she could feel the eyes of those on the patio staring at her. When she finally composed herself, she was stunned to see Wyatt standing directly in front of her. Except for a bit of extra weight around his waist, he still had that air of ego that permeated the entire room. Leave it to him to not only have kept all of his hair, but even though it had gotten darker with age, there wasn't a single gray one on his head.

"Melanie? Are you all right?" Hearing Wyatt say her name sent an involuntary shiver throughout Melanie's body.

"I'm fine Wyatt," she said coolly, "Excuse me, I need to get some water."

Melanie picked up her empty glass and left the patio, all the while mentally reprimanding herself for the way she had reacted. She had been married and divorced twice, and never even thought of those two much more recent relationships once they ended, but for some reason she couldn't seem to stop her body from trembling the moment Wyatt walked into the room. One of the reasons she hadn't attended any of the previous reunions was because she didn't know how she would react to seeing him again. Twenty years or twenty days, it didn't seem to matter where Wyatt Gaynes was concerned. Forgetting about the water,

Melanie headed back out to the bar to refill her drink when Katie met her.

"Mel, isn't this great how many people actually came?"

"Congratulations, Katie. It looks like this weekend is going to be a success after all. I told you not to worry. How is James?"

Out of the corner of her eye, Melanie could see Wyatt in the back of the room, laughing with several of the old cheerleaders. She felt her face flush when she saw him deliberately direct his attention toward her.

"He's doing fine. He should be here any minute. Did you see Eric and Chuck come in together? I saw them talking to Wyatt when he arrived, now he's over there with his usual fan club. I swear, thirty years and he's not changed one bit."

"Well, some of us do actually grow up."

Melanie forced her attention away from Wyatt and back to her friend. "This wine isn't doing a thing for me. I'm going out to get my date, Jack Daniels. See you in a bit."

Melanie found an empty barstool and was relieved to see that Don was still on duty.

"Another white wine?" Don asked when Melanie put her empty glass on the bar.

"No thanks, Don. I need something stronger. Jack Daniels on the rocks, please."

He put a fresh drink in front of her. "J.D. is a strong drink. Must be a strong reason you switched."

"I think it's just this whole high school reunion thing. It always stuck me as odd how we can miss it and hate it at the same time. Sort of like we feel about old lovers. How can you miss someone you absolutely never want to see again?"

"Like that guy you were talking about earlier? Is he the reason for the sudden change in alcohol preference?"

"What makes you say that?"

"Well, you're out here alone and you've switched from wine to bourbon in less than an hour, so I'm guessing a man is probably the reason. Besides, I also noticed, unlike most of the other women here, you're not wearing a wedding ring."

"Dammit, Don. You're either the most observant bartender or the most chauvinistic!"

Instead of answering his question, she decided to redirect the conversation. She picked up his left hand, amazed how strong, yet soft, it felt.

"And you're single as well, I assume."

"You know what they say about assumptions, Mel. I might just not like to wear jewelry, or maybe I find that lovely women looking for a shoulder to unload on, tend to tip a lot better if they think there isn't any competition."

For the first time that evening, Melanie was beginning to enjoy herself, and it wasn't the three drinks she had consumed as much as she was enjoying the company of the person who had poured them. Melanie hadn't noticed before, but she could see an impression of very taut chest muscles beneath Don's bartender suit. She also noticed that his blue eyes sparkled every time he smiled, which was quite often when she caught him looking at her.

He had a strong jaw and a bit of stubble that made him a bit rugged, and if she didn't know better, she could swear he had dimples. She'd already established he was single, she wondered how old he was. She was about to ask when another of her classmates sat down next to her.

"I'll take a Vodka Gimlet, Don. Hi, Melanie. It's good to see you."

"Well, if it isn't my favorite film critic, Stuart Janns. Since you talked me into coming to this thing, you're buying."

"I almost didn't make it, but the film festival ended early, so I got on the first flight out of Aspen and checked in this afternoon. Don handed Stuart his drink and Stuart gave him his credit card. "Put the lady's drink on this, too, Don."

"Well, I'm just glad I never made it on the big screen, as they say. That way I avoided being the topic of one of your reviews. I've read some that were quite scathing," she smiled.

"Melanie is no slouch in the movie business. She's the voice of Maggie Franklin, and a few other animated film characters," Don said to Stuart.

"Don, how did you know that?" Melanie was stunned.

"You must have told me," he stammered a bit in reply.

"No, I told you a story about junior high, but I know I didn't have nearly enough to drink that I'd forget telling you something that confidential about the present. I hope that confidentiality agreement is still in force."

To reassure her, Don made the same phantom zipper gesture he had earlier.

"C'mon Mel," Stuart said, "What's the big deal if Don knows you do voice-over work? When you're as good at what you do as you are, why hide it. Right, Don?"

"For one thing, it's in my contract that I can't reveal to anyone that I'm the voice of Maggie Franklin and for another, Don is a complete stranger."

"Well, I wouldn't go that far. Don's been working here for at least, what is it now, Don, five years?"

"Something like that," Don replied.

"Ok, this is getting a bit weird," Melanie said. "Stu, I thought you told me you haven't been back to Abbeyville in years, and you're talking to Don as if you're old friends. Are you and he...?"

"Involved? No. I'm in a committed relationship." Stuart said.

"And I'm straight and not in a committed relationship," Don added, "But you're right. Stuart and I do know each other. We work together."

"Now I'm really confused. Stuart is a movie critic, and you're a bartender. What do you mean you work together?"

Don started to reply when a hand holding an empty class forced its way between Melanie and Stuart.

"Bartender, pour me something with a little kick, will ya? Scotch, neat."

Wyatt banged his glass on the bar several times, then turned his attention toward Melanie.

"I thought you said you were getting some water, that don't look like water to me."

"Wyatt, are you following me?"

"As a matter of fact, I am. You started coughing and ran out of the room. I wanted to see if you were all right."

Don handed Wyatt his drink without taking his eyes off the interaction between the couple.

"It was just getting a bit too stuffy in there." she started.

"Stuffy? Outside on the patio the one night in Minnesota where there isn't any humidity?"

Wyatt knew that Melanie was lying and he wasn't about to let her off the hook that easily.

"Let's just say it was a long day and I needed some air, ok?"

Melanie's frosty tone was more than enough to chill the scotch in Wyatt's hand, even without any ice cubes. In typical Wyatt fashion, he totally ignored her obvious disdain.

"Sure, so now that you got some air, and a refill, let's go back to the party. We haven't seen each other in years and I'd really enjoy catching up."

"I'm sure you would, Wyatt, but I think I'll just finish my drink right here and catch up with you later."

Like in about another twenty years.

"Later it is," Wyatt put his arm around her shoulder and pulled her closer to him.

"I've really missed you, Mel," he whispered. "Let's not make later too late, ok?"

"Sure, whatever, Wyatt," she shook his hand off her shoulder.

Wyatt picked up his drink, tossed a twenty-dollar bill on the bar and walked back to the party. He never noticed that Stuart was watching his every move from the moment he'd sat down, or that Stuart and Don were exchanging a series of visual signals the entire time Wyatt was talking.

Turning his attention back to Melanie, Stuart said, "Looks like you too are picking up right from where you left off in high school, Mel."

Before replying, Melanie took a large sip of her bourbon.

"Hardly. To tell you the truth, Stu, I was really surprised that Wyatt even bothered to come out here to see how I was, but I guess it's in his nature to pursue the ones who managed to get away."

"No regrets?" Stuart said.

"You're kidding, right? I came out here to get away from him," her annoyance with Wyatt was starting to overshadow her previous enjoyment of the evening. "Then he interrupts our conversation just as you were going to tell me about you and Don working together."

She was about to order another drink when she noticed Don had been replaced by a female bartender.

"Speaking of Don, where'd he go?"

"I think his shift just ended. Tell you what. Meet me in my room, its 212, when the cocktail party is over at eleven and we'll tell you everything."

"We? Who's we? You and Don? Stu, why all the mystery?" she checked her watch. "It's only ten o'clock, I can't wait another hour."

"Well, you're just going to have to," Stuart smiled at her unsatisfied curiosity, "and we also need to convince Katie to join us."

"Katie? Does she know what this is about?"

If Stuart answered in the affirmative, Melanie was going to have a serious talk with her girlfriend.

"No, not yet. But she will. Now, let's get back to the party."

Reluctantly, Melanie followed Stuart back to the ballroom. Katie had left her post and was talking to John and his wife. Not wanting to interrupt their conversation, she tried to find someone else to talk to, but her mind wasn't on catch-up small talk, so she found an empty table and waited for Katie to join her. She didn't have long to wait, as soon as she saw Melanie sitting alone, Katie excused herself and went to join her friend.

"Everyone's been asking where you went. James hasn't called and I'm starting to get a bit worried. Where were you?"

Before she had a chance to explain, Stuart approached them.

"Katie, it's very important that we have with you and Melanie after the party," he said. "Melanie, fill her in. I'll see you two at 11."

The urgency in Stuart's voice made both women nervous.

"What is he talking about?" Katie asked. "Fill me in on what? Who is we and why would I go to his room?"

"I'm as much in the dark as you are, Katie but somehow the bartender is involved as well. If I didn't know any better, I'd swear this is some kind of practical joke. From what I can tell, Don is single, really well-built and totally straight, so what's the worst that can happen?"

"Well, if this is a joke, someone went to an awful lot of trouble on our account. The least we can do is play along, until we find out what Don and Stuart are up to."

Melanie hoped she had convinced Katie to go with her. Fortunately, her friend didn't disappoint her.

"I can think of a lot of things those two might have in mind. Even in a boring town like Abbeyville crimes happen but I'm sure that's not their intent. Besides, I have to admit Stu has me very curious. I'll leave James a message on his cell to let him know where I am," Katie said. "I see a few people are already beginning to leave, so I'll go say goodnight and meet you by the elevator in an hour."

Katie left Melanie alone to contemplate Stuart's mysterious invitation. If Don had asked her to meet him alone that would have been a lot less mysterious then a foursome, especially since one of the four was totally monogamous and the other one was gay. Hopefully, the bartender would bring along a fifth to their little party.

A "fifth" by the name of Jack Daniels.

Chapter Five

As her former classmates began leaving the cocktail party, they each made a stop at the entrance to tell Katie what a great time they had, and how much they were looking forward to the banquet on Saturday. Katie thanked them for attending, then quickly gathered the registration papers and called James to let him know she was going to be home late. When the call went to voice mail again, Katie started to feel an unfamiliar worry knot begin to grow in her stomach. There were many times the legislature would work late, but James always found a way to let her know what time he'd be coming home. If she didn't know any better, she might have suspected he was with another woman.

Katie met Melanie at the elevator and they entered together, but just before the doors closed completely, a man's hand triggered them to reopen. The hand was connected to the body of Wyatt, and his other hand was connected to the waist of the cocktail waitress who had been serving at the party.

"Hi girls. This is, uh . . . " he turned to look at the waitress' name tag, "Cheryl. Say hi to my good friends K.C. and Mel, Cheryl."

"Hi." The waitress was a little shy and appeared to be nearly half their age.

I guess he couldn't wait for later, Melanie thought.

"Robbing the cradle are we, Wyatt?" Melanie whispered her sarcastic question a bit too loudly. Fortunately the elevator stopped at the second floor and the women walked through the open doors before Wyatt had time to reply.

"Can you believe that guy? He's our age and he's still acting like he never left high school," Melanie's disgust was obvious by the tone of her voice.

"You should have heard him tonight, bragging about his stationery store to anyone who would listen. I swear if they took the letter I out of the alphabet, he wouldn't have anything to say!"

"Well, not that I'm trying to make excuses, but I heard he never got over Brenda, breaking their engagement years ago. He's still single and he always comes to events with a different woman on his arm. I think the guy is just lonely."

"Katie, you always did believe the best of people, but in this case, I think you're totally wrong. Wyatt is alone because any woman in her right mind wouldn't be able to put up with his bullshit any longer than one night."

Before Katie could reply, Melanie stopped in front of a door.

"Here it is. Room 212."

Melanie knocked on the door and Stuart let them into the suite. Don was sitting on the couch, surrounded by several unopened file boxes. There were maps laid out on the coffee table and a large white board was behind him.

"Welcome, ladies," he said. "Please make yourselves comfortable. I know it's late, but can I offer either of you a drink? Jack Daniels, as I recall Ms. Tyler."

Don rose from the couch and walked over to the wet bar.

"Now I'm Ms. Tyler? I'll take that drink, thank you Mr.?"

"Wagner. Donald Wagner."

Don answered in a much more formal voice than he used the last time he poured her the drink. "Anything for you, Mrs. O'Brien?"

"No thank you," Katie replied, "Stu, can you please tell us why we're here? I really need to get going."

Katie was becoming irritated. She still had a great deal of preparations to finish before the banquet the following evening and she needed to get a good night's sleep. Melanie took her drink and sat beside Katie on the couch.

"Ok, Mr. Wagner," She said, emphasizing the more formal name. "Will you please explain exactly why you asked us here?"

Instead of replying, Don reached inside his jacket pocket, pulled out a triangular yellow badge with a white numeral 11 printed in the center, and handed it to Melanie. Stu showed Katie an identical badge, only his had a numeral 2 in the center.

"Do you recognize these?" Don said.

"No, not really," Melanie said. "Should I?"

"Mel," Katie said, "You should know what these are. My sons used to play the same game we played when we were their age. These are UNCLE badges."

"From the old television show? You've got to be kidding. Stu, aren't you a bit old to be playing spies?" Melanie giggled and took a sip of her drink.

"I also have this." Stu handed Katie and Melanie his business card. The women started laughing when they saw what was printed on it. The watermark was a blue background with a yellow continent design. In the center there was a round globe with lines crossing through it. It sat on a solid black line, beneath which were the letters; U.N.C.L.E. United Network Command for Law and Enforcement printed on the top line, and beneath was the text: This is to certify that Stuart Janns has qualified for service with UNCLE and may be called to active duty with his/her section on 12 hours notice (Y3K7 - Hazardous Duty).

"Guys, these props must have cost you a bundle. Did you get this stuff on E-bay?" Melanie laughed.

"I'm not in the mood for jokes, Stuart. You know I'm worried about James and you made me stay late for this?" Katie was becoming furious. "I'm going home."

Katie stood to leave and Melanie was about to follow when Don's stern tone stopped them cold.

"Sit down, ladies. I assure you. This is no joke."

"Don. You don't have to frighten them. They have every right to think we're making this up," Stu turned his attention to the women. "Katie. Mel. The truth is, Don and I really are actual agents with the United Network Command for Law and Enforcement, just like the card says. I have been since my first year of college."

"C'mon Stuart. You're a movie critic, for God's sake, you're not a spy. You're gay!" Mel was beginning to feel the effects of the bourbon.

"We're not the military, Mel," Stuart's tone was completely devoid of any humor. "There is no 'don't ask, don't tell' policy in UNCLE, and the agency doesn't discriminate."

"Which is why, if you noticed, there is no silhouette of a man on the insignia."

Don picked up his card and returned it to his jacket pocket.

"You're right, Ms. Tyler, Stuart is a movie critic, which gives him an excellent cover identity so he can travel incognito to all parts of the world on assignment while he's also writing reviews."

"Don. The Man From U.N.C.L.E. was a fictional television show in the sixties. Katie and I just played spies, like I told you, with the guys from our class, but none of it was real. I think you guys are totally nuts."

"You're right about the television show, Ms Tyler..."

"And would you please stop with the Ms. Tyler crap," Melanie interrupted. "I'm sitting in your hotel room, after midnight on a Friday night, getting a bit drunk. I think you can call me Mel, Don."

Melanie not-too-subtly crossed her legs at the thigh. The move didn't go unnoticed by Don. He smiled warmly and continued.

"As I started to say, Mel, you're right about the television show. All those exotic locations were built on a Paramount Studio sound stage and the agents were actors, however, the scripts were all written using specific codes that were transmitted to real agents all over the world."

"You're kidding, right?" Katie was having a difficult time believing what she was hearing, but she was no longer in any hurry to leave.

"That was one of the reasons each episode was called the "such and such" Affair. The title was the key to the code, which was usually integrated into the Solo character's dialogue. The key, as well as the code, was changed each week."

"With the help of the producers and writers, we were able to infiltrate the entire THRUSH organization," Stu added, "Once it was disbanded, we no longer had any need for the television show, so it was cancelled."

"Ok, so let's assume we believe you, which I'm not quite sure I do, that doesn't explain why you're telling us all of this, or why I'm sitting in your hotel room instead of asleep in my own." Melanie was going to add, with Don, but didn't want to upset Katie.

"Or why I'm here instead of at home with my husband!"

Katie was beginning to lose her usual calm demeanor.

"The details are in these files and we'll have more time tomorrow to go over them with you..."

"Tomorrow?" Katie interrupted, "I can't do anything tomorrow, I'm in charge of the entire reunion!"

"We'll meet early in the morning. It won't take more than a few hours to go over everything. I promise you'll have plenty of time to make your reunion," Don said. "Believe me, Katie. After I tell you what is going on, I think you'll agree the situation is a bit more serious than your little party."

"Don," Stu said, "there's no need to be insulting. Just answer their questions."

"I'm sorry, ladies, but we've been trying to infiltrate this guy's operation for so long and now that we're this close, I'm feeling a bit anxious."

"Ok, Don. You talk. We'll listen."

Melanie pretended she was interested in what the men had to say, but all she really wanted to do was appease them so they would finish playing their practical joke and she could leave. It was going to take more than a few trinkets to convince her that any of what Don and Stuart told her was fact.

"First, I need to give you a bit of background information. Abbeyville was just one of many towns where we had satellite operations located in the mid-sixties." Don said. "The agency has been accumulating information for the past thirty years on one of your former classmates and what we believe is an attempt to reorganize Thrush, with their headquarters located right here in Abbeyville."

"We have reliable Intel that something big is going down, but we haven't been able to get any of our people close enough to the head of the operation to get any specific details. We've already lost six agents because the guy became too suspicious, but we figure he'd trust a couple of women from his high school class."

"This thirtieth reunion, by coincidence, corresponded with the date we knew his operation was going on-line," Don added.

"Who is this classmate you're talking about?" Something told Melanie she already knew the answer before Don even said the name.

"Wyatt Gaynes."

"And we also believe that Eric and Charles are helping him." Stuart said.

"You guys are crazy!" Katie jumped up from the couch. "Wyatt isn't the head of any international criminal organization. He owns a stationery store and print shop in town. I don't want to have anything to do with this. I'm going home. Right now!"

"Of course you're free to leave whenever you want," Don said, "but we know why you haven't been able to get in touch with your husband."

Katie's patience was wearing thin. Her usual Minnesotan calm was beginning to turn into a major storm.

"Don, if you know something about James, you'd better start talking and I mean right now!"

Just as he was about to reply, Katie's cell phone rang. "Don't bother, that's his ring tone."

Katie flipped open the phone. Melanie could tell by the expression on her friend's face that Katie was receiving disturbing news. Don and Stuart made themselves busy going over several of the files on the table while they waited for Katie to finish. Fifteen minutes later, Melanie noticed her friend's demeanor was much calmer after she hung up the phone.

"What happened?" Melanie asked.

"That was Frank Campbell, James' chief assistant. Apparently James passed out during the senate vote and was taken to the hospital. They thought he'd suffered a heart attack."

"Heart attack?!" Melanie exclaimed, "Katie, he's only 48!"

"It's okay, Mel. Frank said he's going to be fine. His EKG was normal and they tested him for angina, but his arteries are clear. Frank said he might have something called generalized anxiety disorder, whatever that is. They're releasing him in a few hours, and he'll call me when he gets home."

Stuart said. "GAD is caused by excessive fear and worry and has similar symptoms to a heart attack, like pounding heart, sweating and shortness of breath, but it's not serious."

"That's what Frank said too. I can't imagine what could have caused the attack. I didn't think James was particularly worried about work and he's never been afraid of anything in his life." Katie said, "Although he has been behaving a bit strangely for a few weeks, now that I think about it. Mel knows that James and I have been together for very long time and in all those years, I've never seen him so much as raise his voice let alone lose his temper, but he had been uncharacteristically irritable."

"Go home, Katie," Don tried to show some compassion he wasn't actually feeling. The mission was too important to be compromised by a non-serious medical condition. Stuart scribbled an address on the back of his ID cards and handed one to Katie, and one to Melanie.

"Meet us here at seven o'clock tomorrow morning," he said.

"I can understand why you'd want Katie to help you," Melanie said. "She and Wyatt still live in Abbeyville and she certainly has closer contact with him then I do, so why am I here?

"Melanie, once our agents get everything in place, we're going to need your voice-over skills to set up a fraudulent telecommunications network. Don't worry, you'll both be working with us at UNCLE headquarters far away from any danger."

"And Wyatt doesn't suspect anything?" Katie asked.

"We've got that situation well under control as well," Don replied. "One of our female agents is with him now. Cheryl's mission is to keep Wyatt busy until after the reunion banquet tomorrow night. So, Melanie, Katie, are you two ladies willing to help us nail this guy?"

The room went quiet for several minutes as the women contemplated the agent's offer. Katie thought about how she had always been the strong supporter of her husband and sons as they took center stage. As much as she enjoyed being a behind-the-scenes heroine, this was her chance to do something important on her own. The agents had come to her because of her technical ability and intelligence and not because of her talent as a fund raiser for her boy's sports team, or her husband's campaign.

At her age, she knew this was going to be her first and last chance to accomplish something more important, and a hell of a lot more exciting that baking a Minnesota State Fair red-ribbon winning pie.

"I'd still like to hear more of the details and I'll have to check with James first, of course," Katie said, "but if Melanie agrees, I'm in."

For Melanie, the offer produced quite a different response. The agents only wanted her to do what she was already getting paid to do in her day job. She played many similar roles for the animated characters she gave voices to, so another one or two more wasn't that much of a stretch. What Don and Stuart were asking her to do wasn't anything out of the ordinary, even for a so-called spy mission. Plus spending more time with the handsome UNCLE agent was definitely a very persuasive perk.

"I guess I am too. I'd better get some sleep if we're going to meet up at seven."

"Then it's all set. We'll see you tomorrow morning."

Don was a bit more excited about seeing Melanie then he wanted to admit, or reveal.

"Get some rest. It's going to be a very long weekend."

"You can say that again!" Katie said.

Chapter Six

The women left the hotel room and headed toward the elevator, both silently contemplating what they had just been told.

"I know those two made it all sound very real, but I still don't fully believe Wyatt is some kind of international criminal. A bit full of himself yes, but the new head of THRUSH? Give me a break!"

Melanie followed Katie to the parking lot.

"That's not as hard to believe as it is that Chuck and Eric are part of it. Eric writes for the Wall Street Journal and his partner in crime, so to speak, is the CEO of a mega software company. At least that's what they wrote on their reunion bio," Katie said.

"And I suppose Wyatt's ambition came true if he thought donating millions to the school building fund was his idea of bringing peace of mind to those who needed a new junior high, or maybe it was only seeing his name etched on the plaque in the wall that gave him peace of mind."

The women laughed, which helped release some of the tension each was feeling after their meeting. Just as Katie was about to open the truck door, her phone rang. She indicated to Melanie that it was James and after hanging up, said that he was home, feeling fine and not to worry.

"That's great, Katie. You get home. I'm still a bit too wired to sleep," Melanie said, "and I'm still on California time. It's only eleven o'clock by my watch, I think I'll go for a walk by the lake and clear my head. I guess your prediction in our yearbook actually came true, Katie. After all these years, we're actually working for UNCLE"

"Seems you're right, although I wish you weren't. I'll see you in the morning."

Katie drove out of the parking lot and Melanie walked off in the opposite direction. Following the lights on the path, Melanie spotted a bench by the side of the lake and headed toward it. Even though the Minnesota night air was a comfortable seventy-five degrees, she felt a sudden chill overtake her and she shivered a bit. Although she had agreed to meet Don and Stuart the following morning, she wasn't entirely convinced they were on the level. For all she knew, they could have been involved with Wyatt all along, and the UNCLE story was simply a ruse. If it were all an act set up by Wyatt, why involve Stuart and Katie and the mysterious and interesting Don?

She knew first hand that Wyatt was capable of using people to orchestrate scenarios for his own benefit. Looking out over the lake, Melanie remembered the last time she was in Abbeyville and how Wyatt had done just that. She was going through the first divorce, but made the trip to attend James and Katie's tenth wedding anniversary when James announced his decision to run for public office.

Most of their guests and political supporters were former classmates and residents of Abbeyville, including Wyatt Gaynes. Charming as ever, he insisted on sitting next to her during dinner, joining her on the dance floor and inviting her up to his room for a more private celebration.

Melanie was having too much fun, and perhaps a bit too much to drink and, although she hated to admit it, even ten years after high school, Wyatt's attentions were as intoxicating as the champagne. Later that night in his hotel room, as he held her naked body against him, she had felt such intense passion, she was ready to give up everything if he had only asked. She recalled how his breathing was completely in tuned with hers, until it stopped abruptly, when they heard someone turn the doorknob. She also recalled how Wyatt had jumped off the bed and the look of shock on Brenda's face when she stood there, a bottle of wine in one hand, two glasses in the other, staring at the two of them.

The visual memory of the following scene was a collage of Brenda yelling and Wyatt crying, apologizing and lying, all the while Melanie was trying her best to dissolve into the mattress. She heard Wyatt give Brenda the usual excuses; it wasn't what she thought, he was drunk, he didn't know what he was doing, he loved her more than life itself, he would never do anything to hurt her. Then he'd added another lie that revealed to Melanie what a true bastard Wyatt was; he'd said that Melanie had followed him to his hotel room and that their sexual encounter had been all her idea.

Melanie never forgot the sensation of frost running through her veins where the fires of passion had been only a few moments before. She spent the rest of the night alone in an empty hotel room, waiting for Wyatt to return and explain what had just happened. He never did. Melanie left for Los Angeles on the first flight out of Minneapolis and never told Katie why she didn't stay for Sunday brunch. She hadn't been back to her hometown since.

While she didn't need to be convinced of Wyatt's questionable character, she couldn't believe that even he was capable of pulling off something as elaborate as concocting an entire spy organization or convincing Eric and Charles to help him. As much as she didn't want to believe all that Don had shown them, she had to admit there was an element of credibility if Wyatt Gaynes was involved.

Melanie's thoughts were interrupted by the sound of footsteps approaching. Although she knew Abbeyville was a relatively safe town, after years of living alone in Los Angeles, her immediate instinct was to tense her body and assume a defensive position. She turned toward the sound and once she saw the face of the person was connected to the footsteps, her body remained on alert.

"Hi, Mel. What are you doing out here alone this late?"

"Hello, Wyatt. I could ask the same of you. What happened to your little friend, Cheryl was it?"

Not waiting for an invitation, which Melanie had no intention of offering, Wyatt sat next to her on the bench. He lit a cigarette, took a long drag and simply replied, "She went home. You didn't answer my question."

I'm sitting here thinking what a bastard you were to me and whether or not you're as big a criminal as Don and Stuart told me you were and whether or not I should work with them to destroy you.

"I'm still on California time and couldn't sleep, so I thought I'd go for a walk and ended up here."

"It's good to see you again, Mel. It's been a long time, but you know I think about you often."

Wyatt ran his finger down Melanie's arm shooting a shiver down her spine. It was amazing, Melanie thought, how her body still remembered what her mind so desperately wanted to forget.

"I've thought about you a great deal too, Wyatt. Twenty years is a great deal of time, but it seems as if we only said good-bye to each other last week."

What the hell is wrong with me?

In her career, Melanie spoke for a variety of fictional characters, but now she was hearing words come out of her mouth which she could swear were being spoken by someone else.

"Are you staying in Abbeyville long?" Wyatt asked. "I have some business to take care of, but I would love to spend some time with you. How about tomorrow morning, say around ten or ten-thirty? I could give you a tour of my store, and maybe after the banquet we can meet at my place and put a new definition on the word reunion."

Wyatt placed his finger on her cheek and moved it lightly across her lips. In spite of herself, Melanie's body began to shiver. Thirty years, two thousand miles away and living a completely different life and it only took ten minutes with Wyatt Gaynes to make her feel as if she'd never left Abbeyville. She was closer to fifty then she wanted to admit, but Wyatt made her feel eighteen.

"You do know that I'm here just for the weekend... for the reunion," She said with a shaky voice, "but I'd love to see your store."

His lips were on her neck and Melanie was having a difficult time breathing.

"It will be my pleasure to give you a personal tour of my place. Here's the address," Wyatt handed her his business card, then whispered into her ear, "I really want to finish what we started all those years ago, before Brenda barged into the room."

As soon as Melanie heard him say her name, all of the hurt and pain she had felt that night was instantly brought to the present, and in the present, as in the past, Wyatt Gaynes was a conniving, manipulative bastard. Unfortunately her desire to confirm what Don had told her overcame her desire to rescind her acceptance of his invitation. In a voice that a great deal cooler than it had been moments earlier, she replied, "Then I guess I'll see you tomorrow."

Melanie rose from the bench and started walking up the path leading back to the hotel. With each step she could feel Wyatt's eyes burning into her back like laser beams and she had to force herself not to turn around and return fire. She didn't want to think that somewhere, buried in the cold gray ashes he had left behind from the inferno of their last encounter, there still remained a tiny spark just waiting for Wyatt to light the match and re-ignite the blaze.

Wyatt had used her in high school, caused her emotional pain and walked away unscathed. He had used her again, ten years later, then he'd run out the door and left her alone in an empty hotel room. Then tonight, he simply picked-up right where he had left off, using his boyish charm to make her try to forget all his past transgressions.

There was no longer any doubt in her mind that Wyatt didn't care about the pain he inflicted on Brenda or her, or anyone else. It was beginning to become quite clear to Melanie that as long as he got what he wanted, the only person Wyatt Gaynes cared about was Wyatt Gaynes.

Chapter Seven

Wyatt remained on the bench until he could no longer see Melanie's silhouette. Part of him wanted to follow her, but a much larger part needed to make a phone call and he couldn't take the risk of any distractions, not when there was so much at stake.

Wyatt looked around to make sure he was alone. Satisfied that there wasn't another ear in range, he took his cell from his jacket and flipped open the cover. He paused for a moment to clear his mind from the faint scent of Melanie's perfume, then he pressed the key pad. His head cleared the moment the call connected. Wyatt felt the muscles in his face, which had been so relaxed moments ago, tighten with the seriousness of a man who was not about to let something as trivial as a former fling interfere with his plans.

"Chuck. You'd better have good news for me."

"Of course, Wyatt. I came right to work after the party and found a small glitch. I don't know why it happened."

Chuck tone was more than a little apprehensive.

"I came home to take a quick shower and catch some z's, then I'll head back in a few hours and work on it."

"Chuck, you're going to get that system operational right now. When I told you that you were going to be working through the weekend, I meant you were going to be working through the weekend. I don't care if you have to down ten gallons of coffee, get your ass back there, or else."

Chuck was not about to argue. "Ok, Wyatt. I'm leaving right now."

The phone went dead before Wyatt had a chance to reply. He closed his cell and nearly tossed it into the lake. It had taken him ten years to put his operation together and he'd be damned if he was going to let any one of his players sleep through the most important weekend of his life.

Wyatt had come a very long way since his high school days, and judging from his earlier conversations with the losers of his class, he felt confident that he had surpassed each and every one of them in both money and prestige. Although he put on a humble facade when he talked about his little stationery store and print shop in town, he brilliantly concealed what lie beneath. He was having such a wonderful time pretending to be the same sweet kid of his high school days, he almost began believing it himself.

Sitting alone on the bench, Wyatt looked out over the placid Minnesota lake, the very same lake he had ice-skated on when he was a boy. The very same lake they had found his mother's body floating in the morning of his first birthday. Wyatt learned much later that she had drowned running after him when he had crawled onto the frozen lake. When his mother ran over to pick him up, the ice had given way beneath her.

Wyatt's father, Ted Gaynes grew up on a farm in Marshall, Minnesota, received his Bachelors degree from Minnesota State University, then he went on to Harvard School of Business, where he met Marilyn. Less than a year later, they were married and their first son, Jack was born soon after.

Wanting a better life for his family, Ted sold the farm and they moved to Abbeyville where he decided to invest in a local printing company that specialized in formal invitations. When the owner retired, Ted bought him out and soon expanded the operation to include his own paper mill. The Gaynes Corporation was born two years later, and so was Wyatt. After his wife's death, Ted put all his energies into the company, spending what little free time he had with his first born son. Thousands of dollars of therapy could not alleviate the guilt and unintentional blame Ted bestowed on Wyatt for the loss of his wife.

When Wyatt turned two, Ted felt he was old enough to be told that his mother had died. Wyatt didn't understand what his father meant, having no concept of the word mother. He only knew that the other children he played with had a tall, older woman with them in the park, and at pre-school. He felt that the news should somehow have mattered to him, so he had faked sadness, but in fact, felt nothing at all.

As Wyatt grew up, he could tell that there was something special between his father and older brother. He didn't know what it was, exactly, but he knew he wanted it and would do anything to get it. Ted took Jack with him to work, attended all of his sports events, which his older brother always excelled, but when it came Wyatt's turn, his father was always busy. It seemed to Wyatt the only time Ted notice him was when he was called to the principal's office, which was quite often. And while Wyatt didn't enjoy being punished, he did very much enjoy having his father's complete attention. At least until the yelling stopped.

Wyatt tried to follow in his brother's limelight, but he was just never able to shine the way Jack did in Ted's eyes. At nearly every event during their school's annual all-class Olympics, Jack would end up standing on the highest podium with a gold medal around his neck and there was little brother standing alongside of him wearing the silver. His good friend Stuart thought he could cheer him up by giving him the nickname of Mr. Silver, like a silver fox, but it only made things worse when the rest of the class started calling him Silver Boy.

Wyatt had tried to make a joke of the nickname by calling himself Mr. Silver. He even started using the nickname to entice the cheerleaders, and much to his surprise, it had worked. But he had hated it nonetheless and he vowed to someday get even with Stuart for giving him the loathsome moniker.

As he grew older, Jack and Ted grew closer, leaving Wyatt on his own most of the time. The only friends he had were the guys on the varsity teams, and he knew the only reason they hung around him was the hope they would pick up one of Wyatt's female discards. Wyatt had been fine with that, he had more groupies then he could handle, but the morning Chuck and Eric read Melanie's note in front of his entire entourage was the morning he decided he'd had enough. The boys had totally embarrassed him in front of his teammates and girlfriend and he had to find a way to get back his cool.

Wyatt knew Chuck and Eric were struggling with math and with mid-term exams coming up in a few weeks, he had the perfect solution to regain his reputation. He'd break into the math department, steal the answers and sell them to his classmates. He'd regain their respect and with any luck, will lose that Mr. Silver name for good.

Everything had gone perfectly to plan, until a few days after the transaction when they had told him about what had happened with Katie and Melanie and that James had been the one who had told them about the exams. Of course they hadn't blamed Wyatt, but they did fail their exam and Wyatt was stuck with that awful nickname right up until he walked off the auditorium stage with his diploma in hand. He swore someday he would get even with James O'Brien, no matter how long it took.

If anything positive came out of his high school years, it was his friendship with Melanie Tyler. At first he had felt badly for her for what Eric and Chuck had done, but eventually his feelings began turning into something other than pity. She wasn't the typical cheerleader bimbo he was more than happy to use toss away, but she also wasn't a girl up to his usual standards. So, he would wear a disguise and sneak into the auditorium when she was performing, and after would walk her home under the cover of darkness. She told him she understood, that he had a certain reputation he had to maintain, and she would wait for him to make up his mind.

She was easy to talk to, and Wyatt could totally be himself when he was with her. He thought he could change his ways and he invited her to the Senior Prom. But no sooner had they entered the ballroom, when he saw the stares and heard the whispers coming from all sides of the room that Mr. Silver couldn't get a real date and had to settle for second best. Again.

Wyatt had suggested to Melanie that they move the prom down the road, to a more private room where he proved once and for all that he was good as gold. It wasn't until they were lying naked afterward that she told him she was leaving for California at the end of the week. It was apparent to Wyatt that his making love to Melanie wasn't good enough to change her mind. He dropped her off at her house, said an insincere "I'll call you" and drove away. It would be ten years before he saw her again.

Wyatt spent that summer sifting through dust at his dad's paper mill. Jack was at Harvard finishing his MBA, so Ted thought he'd give his second son an opportunity to see what he was made of by starting him at the very bottom of the mill rung. It didn't take him long to find out that his son had very little interest in any part of the corporate ladder, and less interest in the family business. After years of being ignored by his father, it was quite clear that Wyatt also had no interest in Ted.

Not wanting to completely cut his son out of his life, Ted offered to pay for any college of Wyatt's choosing. Wanting to relocate to a warmer climate, and be as far away from his overbearing father and his disgusting paper mill as he could get, Wyatt decided on the University of Tampa in Florida, an easy liberal arts school where no one would know anything about his brother and Wyatt could finally come out from under Jack's shadow.

Without any authoritative figures to keep him in check, Wyatt received an entirely different education than either his father or brother achieved at Harvard. Wyatt knew his brother was more suited to boring corporate meetings in a business suit then lying on the beach in a bathing suit. He also knew that all work and no play would make him a very dull boy as well, and dull was not something Wyatt Gaynes was famous for. His freshman year he majored in fraternity rush parties 101 and advance keggers.

He soon forgot all about his regular classes. He also forgot the very strict alcohol laws in Florida. When he tried to use fake I.D. to purchase some beer one night, he was sorely reminded.

Being a cute blond Minnesota boy might have been an advantage with college freshman girls, but it was a huge disadvantage in the Florida county jail. What was worse for Wyatt was when he used his one phone call to phone his dad to bail him out, his father told him he was an adult and that it was about time he started acting like one. Ted was adamant that Wyatt take responsibility for his own actions, and told him not to bother showing his face again until he had.

Wyatt was returned to his cell. With no money, or the ability to make another call, he had to find another way to make bail. Wyatt knew he had to rely on his informal education to survive, and the one class he excelled in was the art of bullshit. As soon as the cell door closed behind him, he began bragging to his cell mate, a Cuban national who was caught carrying a counterfeit green card, all about his family's paper mill, trying to convince the man that if he helped him with bail, he would be repaid with interest. As it turned out, his new friend's interest in Wyatt was ten times more than just a return on his investment.

His cell mate's name was Sepheran and he wasn't just an ordinary illegal. He told Wyatt that, in fact, he was one of the last remaining members of an organization known as

THRUSH, The Hedonistic Reformation for the Ultimate Submission of Humanity.

At first, Wyatt thought Sepheran was making up some elaborate story, or that he was totally crazy, but since he was also Wyatt's ticket out of jail, he kept quiet and listened to the rest of what Sepheran had to say. According to his cellmate, THRUSH disbanded in the early 60s, and had become a mere shadow of what they had once been, but recently a few key players had begun to emerge, and they needed a new leader, and a new plan. Sepheran had come to U.S. to meet up with his contacts, but was arrested before he had the chance.

Wyatt was now more than a little intrigued by Sepheran's story. The two men spoke for hours before Sepheran's contact arrived to post bail. Once they were free, Sepheran introduced Wyatt to the other members of what was left of THRUSH. They immediately took to the highly charismatic American and his analysis of their situation. Their individual groups were completely disenfranchised, many had a different set of goals and there was a great deal of infighting. It didn't take Wyatt long to impress what was left of the membership to envision a much more global plan, and to convince the heads of the individual cartels that careful patience and planning was the only way they were going to rise from the ashes, like the another bird, the Phoenix. Sepheran became Wyatt's chief organizer, leaving Wyatt free to return home and establish his base of operations.

Wyatt returned to Abbeyville to collect his trust fund, only to discover it had been dissolved and he was essentially broke. His father had retired and Jack was now CEO of Gaynes Industries. When he asked his brother to let him back into the company, Jack turned him down flat and since Ted no longer had any say in the operation of the company, the best he could do for his son was set him up with a small printing and stationery store in the heart of town. After that, both Ted and Jack pretty much washed their hands of him and Wyatt was free of all family ties and responsibilities.

There were many late night meetings in the basement of Wyatt's store with Sepheran and several of his fellow former operatives and it wasn't long before a solid plan began to come together. However, Wyatt didn't fully trust his new partners, and he knew he needed key players that, at the very least, wouldn't be speaking to each other in a foreign language he couldn't understand. Former friends would be the perfect target, he thought, and his class' tenth reunion would be the best opportunity to discover their weakness and exploit it to his own advantage.

Wyatt began making a list of possible candidates. In the short term, he needed a high profile business reporter to help make his own company profitable. In the long term, he knew he would need an expect computer programmer for his international communications and an influential politician in his back pocket would complete the picture. It hadn't taken Wyatt long to find the reporter, and the others followed soon after.

At the O'Brien's anniversary party reception where the guests mingled, Eric Kramer was more than eager to put Wyatt on the top of his must mingle list. Eric told Wyatt that his journalist career was going no where, even with his Masters degree from the University of Missouri, the only assignments he had been covering were boring dog bites man stories. Eric told Wyatt that he really needed a "big" story which would launch his journalistic career, and thought a national profile on the Gaynes family would be perfect. But instead of asking Wyatt to be the focus of the piece, Eric had asked him to give his card to his brother Jack so he could interview him on running the family business.

Wyatt said he would do what he could, without any intention of doing so. When Eric told him he was leaving for South America to investigate a rumor about a suspected slave trade, Wyatt came up with the perfect plan. Three days later, Wyatt put in a call to his THRUSH contacts in a small obscure village in South America and set-up the fake story for Eric to "uncover".

The expose resulted in Eric receiving the Pulitzer for International Reporting, and a very prestigious job with the Wall Street Journal. At the celebration party, Wyatt had taken Eric aside, showed him the faked documents and threatened to expose him as a fraud.

Soon after, articles about Wyatt's stationery store began being prominently featured in Eric's Man on the Street column, and Wyatt's business began to thrive. That was only the beginning.

Chatting with the other guests, Wyatt overheard talk that James O'Brien was thinking about running for a seat on the city council. Always one to help an old friend, Wyatt offered to sign on as James' campaign manager. The deal was signed with a handshake, and soon after Wyatt set up James' campaign office, hired his staff and set up all of his campaign financial records. Wyatt also created two nearly identical reports, one for the elections commission, the other for himself.

Wyatt was building his worldwide operation, bit by bit. When the new Millennium began, his portfolio was only slightly financially affected by the dot.com crash of 2001. However that gave him the much needed final piece to his plan. Wyatt needed an expert computer geek to finish the final programming, and who better than an old friend who was facing financial ruin.

Charles Haussman was living in Silicon Valley when his financial empire came crashing down. His son was in his second year of medical school at Stanford and his daughter had applied to Princeton. Charles was desperate, and a desperate man was an easy target. With his financial situation precarious, Charles was very surprised when his daughter ran into his office all excited that she not only was accepted in the college of her choice, but had also received a fully paid scholarship for the entire four years. Soon after, Charles received a notice from Stanford that his son's entire medical school expenses had been paid in full.

What Charles didn't know, until much later, was that Wyatt's operatives had hacked into the admissions office of Princeton and made sure Charles' daughter was accepted. He also arranged for full tuition to be paid at both colleges. Then, Wyatt had flown to California, under the pretense he was visiting the local wineries and wanted to look up his old friend. Charles was very glad to see his old high school friend, until Wyatt showed Charles him the paperwork and simply told him that unless Charles agreed to come work for him, the money would be withdrawn and he's reveal the falsified admissions. Once that happened, that would be the end of med school for Charles's son and his daughter would be expelled, not only Princeton, but no other university would take her. The threat was all he needed to convince Charles to agree to join Wyatt's newly organized THRUSH.

Charles packed up and moved from the warmth of California to the frigid Minnesota tundra. Charles's wife lasted one winter before leaving him, but Charles had no choice but to stay and finish the job for Wyatt, at least until his children graduated.

Now, Wyatt's plan was finally coming together. One more day and he'd own this stupid little town, he thought, and his brother, Brenda and all the others who had said he was only second best would know he had made it to the top. There was only one person whom he wished could have been with him at his moment of triumph.

When he saw Melanie at the cocktail party, his first instinct was to greet her with a hug, but then he remembered what happened the last she was in his embrace, and decided against it. Twenty years might not have been nearly enough time for her to forgive him for what he had done which was quite obvious when he felt the chill in the air between them drop below zero before the last syllable of his ex's name escaped his lips.

He wished that he had the chance to tell her that he had returned to the hotel room that night only to find out Melanie had already left. If she hadn't, Wyatt would have told her the real truth of the events of that night that Wyatt had meticulously planned for his girlfriend to walk in and discover him in bed with another woman to make her jealous. The way Brenda made him feel every time she mentioned his brother.

Before he left Florida, Wyatt played the part of party boy nearly every night, until he met Brenda. She was a cocktail waitress in a local hang-out which he frequented. It didn't take long for his charm to win her over, and they began dating regularly. When they'd returned to Abbeyville two weeks before Katie and James' anniversary party, Wyatt mistakenly introduced Brenda to his brother. After that, Jack was all Brenda could talk about, what Jack was wearing at the company party, the gorgeous house that Jack lived in, and what a great success Jack was at running the family business compared to Wyatt's endless series of failures.

Wyatt was at the end of his patience. He didn't want to break up with Brenda, but he needed to shut her up about Jack and find a way to make her see that it was Wyatt she really loved. The best way to do that, Wyatt thought at the time, was to make Brenda believe that another woman wanted him. At first he had planned on hiring a hooker, but once he saw Melanie at the O'Brien's party, he set her sights on her instead. Wyatt rationalized that since Melanie lived in California, and it was only going to be a one-night thing, he was sure Melanie would understand. Fortunately for Wyatt she had been a willing participant.

It hadn't taken much more than a phone call, and a promise of a romantic overnight at one of Abbeyville's most prestigious hotels to entice Brenda to meet him in the hotel room at the exact time where she would be certain to discover him in bed with Melanie. Unfortunately, Wyatt had underestimated Brenda's reaction. Instead of falling for his pretense, and his overblown apologies, she had run straight into his brother's waiting arms

They married the following year.

Wyatt wasn't invited to the wedding, but by that time he was too involved with setting up the final pieces of his organization to care.

When he saw Melanie sitting alone on the bench, it had been so easy to fall back into his old routine, and he momentarily regretted it, but she didn't seem to notice, or maybe after all these years, she simply didn't care, he thought. But, she did take his card and Wyatt was confident that she'd call him, and maybe they would pick up where they had left off all those years ago. Afterall, she was here, she was alone, and she was still very attractive. What better way to spend an otherwise boring reunion than with a familiar body? He could feel their very unique passion begin to stir within him when their lips had met, even for a brief time. All he needed to do was turn up the heat a bit and she'd melt back into his arms, and into his bed, whichever he desired, but that scenario would have to wait.

Another time, another place, he thought as he rose to return to his car for the drive home. He was determined not to let anything, or anyone, not even a former lover, stand in his way.

Yes, Wyatt felt very confident. He took out a cigarette and began to relax for the first time in months. After twenty-five years of planning all the pieces were now in place. It had been a long time coming, and a great deal of planning and hard work, but by this time Sunday night, Wyatt would finally achieve everything he had ever wanted. Nothing less than total control over the entire world.

With the headquarters right in his tiny innocuous hometown of Abbeyville, Minnesota.

Chapter Eight

At seven o'clock Saturday morning, a very tired Melanie met her girlfriend in front of the Center Bakery, which was located, not coincidently on Center Street, one of the two main streets that ran through the heart of Abbeyville. The other, of course, was Main Street.

Melanie was astonished at how rundown her hometown had become since the last time she had visited. Katie had told her that a number of farms in the area had failed and families were moving to Minneapolis or Duluth, leaving much of the town with boarded up windows and empty parking lots. The biggest hit the town had taken was when Jack moved the Gaynes Corporation headquarters to Makato shortly after his father died. Once the plant shut down, the next biggest employer closest to Abbeyville was the Minnesota state correction facility in Moose Lake.

After Minnesota legalized Indian gambling, James had tried to convince his fellow city council members that having a casino in town would bring in much needed revenue. For a time the idea sparked some interest in investors, several of whom were responsible for renovating the now luxurious Abbeyville Hilton, but Katie told Mel that once James left for the capital, enthusiasm for the casino project all but vanished, and now she didn't think that the town would ever return to what it once was. It was a shame, Melanie thought, that memories would be the only things left of a once thriving community.

As soon as they opened the bakery door, smells of freshly baked bread and donuts ignited those very memories in the minds of both women. Katie recalled neighbors bringing warm rolls to Sunday breakfast before church, and the many joyous celebrations shared over exquisitely decorated cakes. For Melanie, the aroma reminded her of the more turbulent time when the neighbors brought those same breads and rolls to her family's home the day they received word her brother was not returning from his tour of duty in Vietnam.

Melanie forced the painful mental images from her mind. They entered the bakery in time to see Don and Stuart emerge from behind the counter. The men greeted the women warmly, handing each of them a blueberry muffin, and indicated they should follow them into the back.

"Ladies, what we're about to show you, you will not be able to reveal to anyone. Not even your husband, Katie," Don said.

"Don, I'm not in the habit of keeping secrets from James. We were up late last night after he came back from the hospital. He looked fine, just really tired. He was still sleeping when I left this morning, or else I'm not sure I would have been able to do this. I just have to remember to bring him some coffee buns since that's the excuse I'll use when I get home."

Katie was starting to become irritated. She still had a great deal to do before the reunion banquet that evening and she wasn't totally convinced that Don and Stuart were telling the truth. Until they reached the back of the bakery.

"So, this is where they make all that great stuff," Melanie said, looking around at the huge mixers and cake decorating tables. "Ya know, L.A. has some great food, but nothing that ever comes close to home. Look at those bags of flour, they must be piled ten feet high."

"Looks can be deceiving," Stuart said as he raised the label on one of the flour bags, to reveal an electronic key pad beneath. He pressed several buttons and an entire row of flour bags slid to the side revealing a hidden elevator.

"You have got to be kidding me!" Melanie said. "How long has that been there?" She asked.

"UNCLE's Midwest headquarters has been here since the mid-sixties. This was built during the Cuban Missile crises. If you ladies would please follow us."

Don and Stuart stepped into what appeared to be an elevator. Once the women joined them, Don pressed the button and they watched as the elevator door, or in this case, the fake stack of flower bags, closed.

"Now, are you convinced that we're telling the truth, Katie?" Stuart said.

"I'm starting to, but you'll have to do a lot better than fake bags of flour," Katie said. "Mel, you've been rather quiet, what do you think about all of this?"

"It's pretty impressive, but I still have no idea what you expect us to do," Melanie said. "We're so not in high school anymore. Hell, I'm going to be fifty years old in a couple of years. Don't you think we're a bit too old to be playing spies?"

"Didn't you hear? Fifty is the new thirty." Don smiled, then became more serious. "Mel, if we were only playing a game, I'd agree. Unfortunately it's anything but. C'mon, ladies, we're here."

The elevator stopped and the four exited into an ultra modern office suite. The receptionist handed Don and Stuart yellow triangular badges, the women received red ones.

"These will give you access to the entire operation," she said. "You are now official temporary agents of the United Network Command for Law and Enforcement. We have a great deal to do and not a lot of time, so if you'll follow the boys, we'll get started."

"Sure, we'll follow the boys." Melanie giggled.

The women walked with Don and Stuart as they past several thick mahogany doors with only gold numbers embedded into the center.

"Don't let the opulent looks fool you, ladies. These office doors are bullet-proof and enforced against nearly all types of explosives."

"That's reassuring," said Katie.

"It's the nearly I'm concerned with." Melanie said.

Don laughed and continued with the tour.

"Each number signifies a different section of the operation," He pointed out each door as they walked by. "Section 1, Policy and Operations, where the assignments are handed out. You already know Stu and I work in section 2,as do all senior agents, Operations and Enforcement. Section 3 is Enforcement and Intelligence where the junior field agents begin their assignments after they've completed their training. You'll be working in Section 4, Katie, Intelligence and Communications, where all the computers are located and Melanie will be in Section 5 Communications and Security."

"Let me guess, that's where you keep the communication devices, like telephones."

Mel was beginning to feel that Don was being a bit patronizing.

"Among other things, like our satellites, cell towers, and covert listening devices," Don continued, unfazed. "Section 6, Security and Personnel. It's also the medical section that handles injuries, and Section 7, Public Relations."

"It used to be called Public Relations and Propaganda," Stuart added, "But after the cold war ended there was no need for that department."

"And what, exactly does your public relations department do in a highly secret organization?" Melanie asked.

"They do their best to keep it that way. We have a great team of very imaginative people who can come up with an alibi and plausible explanation for just about any situation."

"If they ever wanted to change jobs, I'm sure there are many openings for their talents at the state capital," Katie said.

"Or Washington!" Mel added.

"I'm sure some of those politicians could also use Section 8, Deception and Camouflage," Stuart joked.

"You got that right, just ask Mark Sanford or John Edwards," Katie laughed.

"UNCLE doesn't get involved with political or personal scandals," Stuart said. "If we did, we'd need around five hundred more agents."

"At least." said Don. "Ok ladies, now that the official tour is over, we'll begin the briefing."

Don opened the door marked 1 and the women followed him and Stuart into a conference room where, just like the television show, there was a huge round table in the middle of the room. On the table were several files, and other items the women recognized, especially the guns.

"Hey, is this what I think it is?" Katie picked up a thin silver pen.

"Yes, that's a real communicator pen. Cell phones are too much of a security risk, and shoe phones are just not practical. That was a joke, ladies."

"We still use the cigarette case communicator, but not too many of our agents carry them since no one really smokes anymore," Stuart added.

"Really?" Melanie took out her own cigarette case, opened it offered one to Don.

"No, thanks, Mel. I gave them up years ago, they're bad for your health."

"Oh, and having people shoot at you isn't?" Melanie returned the cigarette case to her purse. "I don't really smoke, either, unless I'm really stressed, like now."

"Well, just for you, take this," Stuart said.

He handed Melanie an innocent looking silver case, then slid over a latch, exposing the electronics on the inside.

"This is the transmitter."

Stuart pressed a button and it lit up a small opening in the top.

"It even has a built-in lighter, and if you need it, the cover pulls off and becomes a very sharp blade, so be careful."

"I'm looking at major weapons here, and you're concerned about a little knife? Nice."

Melanie took the case from Stuart.

Don handed the women each a pen then showed them how to activate it by twisting the middle and raising the antenna.

"When the communicator is on, the light in the antenna will flash," he said, "Once the pen is activated, just say open channel D, tell the operator your code names, Melanie yours is M9, Katie your is K..."

"Don, don't you dare tell me that my code name is K9!" Katie remarked.

"No, Katie, UNCLE doesn't have that kind of sense of humor. Yours is K.C., like when we were in high school," Stuart said.

"Oh NO, Stu. I'd rather have K9," Katie said.

"Don't worry, Katie. If everything goes according to plan, neither one of you will have to use the pen or your code name, but you should both put the UNCLE emergency phone number on speed dial just in case."

The women entered the numbers into their address book. Answering their question before they asked, Don said, "We don't give out agents' private numbers since cell tower signals can be very easily monitored. The transmitters in these babies are linked only to our satellite. The signal is so strong that it can penetrate concrete and steel from a mile below ground. Not that I'd ever want to test that theory," he said.

"All of this equipment is top secret, so you both have to swear not to use them in front of anyone."

"We understand."

"No, I don't think you do. You have to swear, literally." Don handed them each a three-by-five-card. "Just read the oath written on the back. It's short, but it's legally binding."

"Like my marriage vows?" Melanie said, "We all know how those worked out."

"Yes, but in this case should you break your vows, someone will probably break your neck. Katie, if you don't think you can keep this from James, then walk away now."

"Is my being part of this really that important?" Katie asked.

"If it wasn't, we wouldn't have asked you to join us. We found out that Wyatt's plan is going down Sunday and there isn't any time to train another agent."

"Sunday? This Sunday? How are we supposed to get this done by tomorrow? I have a reunion banquet to run tonight!" Katie was becoming hysterical. "Not to mention the reunion brunch after church."

"Relax, Katie," Stuart said. "If everything goes according to plan, and we have no reason to suspect it won't, you'll be out of here in time for the second morning mass at ten a.m. and plenty of time to make your reunion brunch."

"And just what role am I supposed to play in all of this? I'm no computer whiz." Melanie said.

"No, we need Katie for that. Your skills lie in other areas," Don started.

"Hey, just wait a damn minute there, bud," Melanie protested.

"That's not what I meant, Mel," Don smiled. "First, take the oath, then we'll go over the plan in detail."

The women didn't need to read the words on the card, they both had them committed to memory. They were the exact same words they had James recite in Melanie's basement all those years ago. As soon as they had finished the oath, the lights went out and a screen appeared on the back wall.

"Please take a seat, ladies, the show is about to start. Sorry we don't have any popcorn," Don smiled.

Although she was feeling a bit apprehensive, Melanie couldn't help also feeling a certain comfortable warmth generating from his smile.

After everyone was seated, Stuart hit a switch on the console and a schematic of Abbeyville high school appeared on the screen. The classrooms were color coded and labeled with various organizational specialties.

"As I mentioned, UNCLE was located in small towns all over the U.S. Contrary to the television show, we purposely avoided major cities like New York or Los Angeles, because they would be obvious targets, so we set up operations in places that no one would suspect," Don began.

"Abbeyville was certainly a town no one would notice," Melanie said.

"Right. The best place for our operatives to hide in plain sight was right here at our high school," Stuart continued. He hit the switch again and a series of faces appeared in an organization flowchart.

"There are the UNCLE field agents. The man at the very top of the chart is Joshua Lawrence. He's the head of this division."

"I see you and Stuart's faces are on the second level. That's pretty high up on the food chain, isn't it?" Melanie asked.

"When you've been doing this as long as we have..." Stuart said.

"And if you're still alive..." Don added.

"And if you're still alive," Stuart echoed. "The higher up on the level, the more security clearance you have. It took us more than twenty years to reach the top tier."

"And we lost a lot of good men and women on the way, but it's not a good idea to dwell on that right now. I'm sure you recognize some of the faces on the lower tiers."

"I think you both remember these people from our high school days," Stuart said as several faces appeared on the screen. "Vince Alessio, our gym teacher was a martial arts expert. David Williams, the sixties hippy, walked with a limp from a wound he'd received stopping a bombing while working undercover with the SDS."

Another photo appeared on the screen.

"Chemistry teacher Martin DeGatto, you can probably figure out he was our bio weapons expert."

"I sure remember Doc. He was such a hunk. I think every girl in school had a crush on him," Melanie said. "I also remember the guy in the photo underneath. He was our English teacher, Anthony Croitz. We heard he was killed in a weird car accident."

"Yes, it was weird, but it wasn't an accident. Tony had just decoded a transmission and was on his way to headquarters to deliver it when THRUSH hit his car with a heat sensor missile."

"Wow. I'm stunned." Katie said.

"And of course one of our first female agents back in the 80's, Gayle McGee. She was working at the radio station when she was killed by a THRUSH agent who she found out was trafficking drugs for a record producer and laundering the money through the radio station's chief engineer."

"Everyone thought she fell out of her apartment window." Melanie said.

"Yes, that was the cover story," Don turned on the lights. "Now, we come to why we're here. Or, more important, why the two of you are here."

"Other than the fact we're two old broads from Minnesota who used to play spies and we work cheap?"

"Speak for yourself, Katie," Melanie said. "I'll have you know I get paid... well, never mind what I get paid. Go on, Don. Why exactly does an international organization of professional spies need us?"

"Well, for one thing, we are an organization of professional spies, as you so eloquently put it, which is why no one from our agency has been able to get close enough to the head of THRUSH to take any significant action." Stuart replied.

"As we told you, Wyatt is extremely suspicious of strangers. Even one of our best operatives, Cheryl, didn't last through one night. It would take months for one of us to get close enough to be effective, and we don't have that kind of time."

"What we do know about Wyatt is that he wouldn't have the same security in place for a couple of women he grew up with. Especially if one of them was a nice church-going PTA mom."

"Thanks a lot, Stu," Katie said, indignantly.

"There's nothing wrong with that, Katie."

Don felt a bit of resentment in Katie's voice and wanted to make it disappear as quickly as possible. There was a great deal to do, and not very much time to get it all done. Stuart unintentionally insulting Katie wasn't the real issue. It was Melanie's role in the mission which Don had to be very careful to explain. He decided to use as few words as possible.

"And the other was someone who Wyatt had, at one time, been romantically involved," he said.

"Well, I wouldn't go that far," Melanie said. "I don't consider what we had, or rather didn't have, exactly a romantic involvement. It was more like a train wreck."

"Nonetheless, as Stu said, you two are the last people Wyatt would ever expect to be UNCLE agents. Our Intel discovered that he called a meeting of his top operatives that will take place tomorrow night. If our plans are successful we'll finally be able to put him, and his entire organization away for a very long time. Ladies, I think you both know the number one man at the head of the new THRUSH organization."

The lights went out once again, and on the screen appeared the smiling face of Wyatt Gaynes.

Chapter Nine

Wyatt's photo showed a man with a very warm smile but whose eyes were devoid of any emotion. Melanie noticed that his hair was cut far too short, making his ears appear to stick out and his head awkwardly disproportionate from the rest of his body.

"Yup, that's Wyatt all right. No one has a bigger head," Melanie giggled.

"Wyatt was always trying to live up to his brother's success and always falling short. He's spent most of his life trying to get out from under that "Silver Boy" label I gave him in high school," Stuart explained. "It seemed that everything his brother Jack touched turned to gold, while everything Wyatt put his slimy fingers on turned to ashes."

"And he never took responsibility for his failures as I recall," Melanie said. "Wyatt always had some rational excuse for his shortcomings and they were always someone else's fault. Even while playing high school sports. If he missed a basket, he'd say the floor was too slippery. Miss a forward pass and it was the quarterback's bad throw, or sun got in his eyes. Have a sexual indiscretion and it was the woman who came onto him, he was just an innocent bystander."

Melanie tried not to remember that very personal excuse she had experienced first hand.

"I remember he was always getting into trouble with the police for one thing or another," Katie said, "And his daddy would always show up to rescue his prodigal son. I don't think his father was doing him any favors."

"Yes, it's not a pretty story."

Melanie was starting to feel a bit of sympathy for the boy she thought was her friend. A boy whose body was still very much alive, but whose soul had died a very long time ago.

"Or, a pretty picture for that matter," Katie said, pointing to Wyatt's photo.

"That's for sure." Melanie sighed.

Don continued with the briefing.

"We were still watching the Gaynes paper mill and unfortunately we weren't paying too much attention to Wyatt."

"That was your first mistake." Melanie said.

"We know that now, but back then the only thing we knew was that Wyatt returned to Abbeyville a few years after Ted retired and opened a print shop and stationery store in the heart of town. Above ground it was a nice little retail establishment, and below ground, although we didn't know it at the time, Wyatt was rebuilding THRUSH"

The image on the screen changed to a man with very dark features and small, deep set eyes. Neither woman recognized him, but they both found the image to be quite threatening

"This is Sepheran. We never found out if that was his first or last name. He was the last remaining leader of the old THRUSH organization and Wyatt's right hand man, until his body washed up on Cap d'Agde in France a few years ago."

"Don, you don't think Wyatt had anything to do with his death do you?" Melanie said.

"Not unless Wyatt had a passion for nude beaches," Don smiled. "No, our agents didn't find anything suspicious, at least nothing connected to Wyatt."

He hit the button again and the faces of Charles and Eric appeared underneath Wyatt's.

"As we've mentioned, these two have been working with Wyatt for a number of years. You can read the details on pages 27 and 35 when you have time."

"When, exactly will that be?" Katie said sarcastically.

Ignoring her comment, Don continued.

"In January of this year, the Euro became the chief currency in thirteen European countries. It's taken Wyatt all this time to collect the right paper, machinery and the right ink to perfect the method to counterfeit, not only U.S. currency, but all of the new Euro paper money as well."

"Stu, this is unbelievable," Melanie said. "I knew Wyatt was a deceitful creep, but I thought that he restricted that character trait to his relationships with women. This elevates him to an entirely different level of bastard."

"We should have known that when we caught him with those stolen math tests all those years ago," Katie said. "And that includes his two co-horts."

Katie's voice didn't hide her contempt. "I would have expected Chuck to have a bit more integrity. I really feel sorry for his wife and kids."

"Don't feel too sorry, Katie. Charles is the computer expert whose program you're going to hack for us," Stuart said.

"Thanks for the vote of confidence, Stu. If what you say is true about Wyatt, this sounds very dangerous."

"Don't worry," Don said, "You'll be working inside UNCLE headquarters with me. It's perfectly safe."

"I'm still not so sure," Katie said. "I know Wyatt's not the most honest guy in the world, but you haven't shown me any evidence he's actually hurt anyone. I can understand why you would want to put all of them in jail, Don and I hate to sound selfish, but all of this really doesn't have anything to do with me."

"You're not being selfish Katie, and we completely understand," Don said. "But there is one more player in Wyatt's game we haven't shown you yet."

Don hit the button on the console and the faces of Charles and Eric were replaced by a 2000 re-election campaign poster of Minnesota State Senator James T. O'Brien.

Chapter Ten

"Don!" Katie screamed. "What is James doing up there? You can't possibly believe he's involved with anything illegal!"

"I'm sorry to have to show you this, Katie," Don motioned to the file in Katie's hand, "Look at page twenty-seven of the file. Gaynes was your husband's campaign manager and he was also in control of the contributions and fund raising."

Katie turned to the pages and began reading the agent's report and Don continued.

"Gaynes knew he needed political influence. There were many permits that needed approval in order for him to build the type of operation he needed. His plan was to find something in the background of his old classmate James O'Brien that he could use against him, but no matter how deep he dug, he couldn't find anything on James he could use, because, frankly, there wasn't anything to find."

I told you so, Katie thought.

"Gaynes only had to entice your husband to throw his hat into the political arena, which he managed to do at your tenth anniversary party. All it took was a Minnesotan gentleman's handshake and a half a million dollars worth of campaign contributions were pledged to James' campaign. Once Wyatt convinced your husband to run for State senate, it didn't take any arm twisting for him to convince James that Wyatt was an expert on the Minnesota elections code and he'd be more than happy to be his campaign manager."

"James and I both totally trusted Wyatt," Katie cried.

"That's what he was counting on," Stuart said. "The only thing that Wyatt told James that was true was that he was an expert on the code, which was how he was able to make certain several of them were violated. Wyatt kept the truth hidden until he could use it to his own advantage."

"Don, this is a load of crap," Katie exclaimed. "It's true that Wyatt worked on James' campaign, but if there was anything illegal going on, why didn't your agency do something about it before now?"

"UNCLE doesn't have any jurisdiction over Minnesota's campaign finance board, but there were several red flags that kept popping up, enough so to draw our interest about five years ago."

"When you moved to Abbeyville, Don." Melanie was beginning to put the pieces together, and the picture wasn't very pretty.

"That's right, Mel. Then Stu called from Paris a few months after I arrived here and asked to come on board. We've been watching Wyatt very closely ever since."

"Katie, you know that all of us go way back," Stuart said, "We've been friends, or at least close acquaintances, since Kindergarten. I wanted, rather I needed to be assigned to this case to protect you and the people we grew up with who still live in Abbeyville just in case what we suspected was true."

"Not to mention the rest of the world," Don added half jokingly.

"Yes, them too."

Stu picked up on his partner's attempt to lighten the mood. The last thing that he wanted to do was hurt his good friend, but it was time for Katie to learn the truth. He could see the sadness in her eyes and he tried to soften the pain of what he was about to tell her. He knew that it wasn't going to be easy.

"Katie, we don't have any evidence that your husband, personally was involved in any illegal activities, however he has been involved with Wyatt since he started his political career back in 1982. After I arrived, I went through all of his campaign's financials and discovered some questionable activities."

"Exactly...how...questionable, Stu?" Katie's voice was full of anxiety. It took all of her self-control just to put a few words into a complete sentence.

"Relax, Katie," Stuart put a reassuring hand on hers. "A few weeks ago, I went to see James and we had a long talk. He told me that at first he had trusted Wyatt and never questioned where the money was coming from, or checked that the reports that needed to be filed with the board were correct," Stuart said.

"As it turned out, Wyatt was keeping his nefarious accounting practices hidden until he felt it was to his advantage to reveal to James what he'd been doing. If the truth had gotten out James knew it would have ruined his career, and might have even sent him to jail, so James felt that he didn't have a choice but to do what Wyatt asked him."

"And what did Wyatt ask him to do?" Katie's face had gone as white as her hair.

"Don't worry, Katie. James is much too decent to cross the legal line," Melanie tried to reassure her friend, but with everything else the agents had shown them, even she wasn't so sure.

"At first it was only a few minor favors when James was on the City Council like convincing the school board to name the new middle school building after Wyatt after he'd made a substantial donation, and passing a re-zoning ordinance when Wyatt wanted to expand his printing operation into a retail store zone. But once James was elected to State Senate, the favors became a lot greater."

"Stu, I'm not sure I can take much more of this."

"I'm sorry, Katie, but you need to know. I think I know why James had that anxiety attack earlier."

Katie closed her eyes and took a deep breath. "I'm all right, Stu. Please continue."

"As we said, in January of this year, the Euro became the chief currency in thirteen European countries. It's taken Wyatt all these months to perfect the computer software and manufacture the plates, he only had one hurdle, Katie, and that's where your husband comes in."

Katie could feel her stomach tighten.

"A bill was introduced that would have banned a specific toxic dye from being imported into the state. Wyatt needed that bill to fail because that was the specific chemical he needed for the imprinting of the counterfeit bills."

"It failed by one vote," Don said.

"James' vote? I don't believe it."

"Believe it, Katie. After our initial meeting, I didn't hear from James again, so we thought his involvement with Wyatt had come to an end, but obviously we were wrong."

"If any of this became public, James' political future would be over," Katie could no longer hold back the tears.

Melanie took a tissue from her purse and handed it to her friend. At that moment there wasn't another human being on the planet she hated more than Wyatt Gaynes.

"We also think that the stress caused your husband's anxiety attack, but you'll have to talk to him about the details. We do understand that you have to discuss all of this with James before you agree to be part of this operation, but we won't be able to pull this off without your help. You'll both have plenty of back-up, myself and Don, plus about fifty other UNCLE field agents, so you won't be in any danger."

"One question, Don," Melanie asked. "If you know all of this about Wyatt, why haven't you arrested him?"

"Up until now, he's been very careful. Besides we don't want to run the risk of filing smaller charges and not be able to prove them when what we really want to do is bring down his entire international network." Don said.

"Wyatt's activities have stopped just shy of breaking any laws, and although we have suspected his involvement in illegal activities, no agency has ever been able to link him directly to anything," Stuart added.

"I'll talk to James, and once he's confirmed what you've told me, I'll do whatever you want to bring Wyatt to justice," Katie said.

"Katie, we know you can take apart and put together any electronic device from the ground up," Don said. "This is what we need you to do."

The image on the screen changed to show a set of schematics and the floor plan of Wyatt's store.

"After our agents infiltrate Wyatt's operation tonight, they're going to re-wire his entire telephone system so that all his outgoing calls come through to this office. That's where your voice-over expertise will be put to use, Mel. Wyatt will think he's calling his contacts, but in fact he'll be talking to you. Once we have the numbers he's phoning, we'll be able to locate all of his other operatives and our international agents will go in and close them down."

"When will we be doing this?" Melanie asked.

"We think Wyatt will be calling his network tomorrow morning. Now here's the tricky part, Mel," Stu began. "We were hoping that Cheryl would have been able to get close enough to Wyatt to keep him distracted, but apparently that didn't work out."

"You mean he pulled the typical Wyatt came and went move, correct? I bet he didn't even bother to take his socks off."

Melanie was pleased that she knew a bit more of Wyatt's M.O. than either of the agents. She wasn't all that pleased to remember exactly how she knew.

"That's correct. Cheryl wasn't all that happy that she failed either. So, now our major problem is how to keep Wyatt from going home after the reunion banquet tonight. If he leaves before our agents have enough time to connect all of his systems to ours, the whole mission will be a failure," Don said. "We need to go to plan B."

Both Stuart and Don turned their attention toward Melanie.

"What are you guys looking at me for?" she began.

"We saw the way Wyatt was looking at you last night at the bar, Mel," Don was hoping she didn't hear any hint of jealousy in his voice.

"I know you and Wyatt were a bit more than friends in high school," Stuart added. "We don't have time to try and find another female agent to get close enough to Wyatt. We need someone he's already close to, someone he trusts who can successfully distract him. And obviously that's not Katie."

"Distract him? Just how do you suggest I do that?" Melanie didn't like what Stuart was implying. She thought she was long past having to use her sexuality for ulterior motives. Apparently, she was wrong. Stuart validated her suspicions with his next sentence.

"Use your imagination, Mel. I think you know, maybe more than anyone, how Wyatt is with women."

"Unfortunately, I suppose I do, but you know Wyatt and I didn't exactly part on the best of terms. Do you think he'd actually believe I was still interested in him after all these years?"

"He's Wyatt Gaynes," Katie said. "He believes every woman is interested in him at any year."

Melanie laughed.

"You want me to keep him busy all night?" she said.

"That's the plan," Don was starting to wish he had come up with a different plan.

"Just long enough for our agents to gain access into his operation so Katie can complete her part of the mission," Stuart said.

"We're not pimps, Mel. We would never ask a non-operative to comprise her, well, you know what I mean."

"Don't worry, Don. I'm a very good actress, and I have ways of keeping a man, uh, distracted as you said. As far as protecting my virtue, believe me, I have had no intention of having sex with Wyatt."

I'd rather make love to you. The thought popped into her head before she had a chance to stop it.

"That's good to know," *really good to know,* he thought, "but just in case things go a bit too far with Wyatt and you don't want to continue, take this."

Don reached into his pocket and handed her a small capsule.

"What's this? Poison, I hope?"

In spite of the seriousness of their plan, Don couldn't suppress a grin.

"No, it's not lethal. We call it simply Capsule C. It's just a knock-out drug. Capsule B induces amnesia, but we can't have Wyatt forgetting his own operation if we're going to be successful in destroying it. Open the capsule, empty it into his drink and Wyatt will pass out in minutes. Just be sure he's sitting on something comfortable, because if he falls down, you won't be able to get him up."

"I thought that's what I was suppose to do." Melanie couldn't help laughing.

In spite of himself, Don laughed also, then his training brought him back to the seriousness of the mission.

"Call us when he leaves in the morning and then come directly back here. We'll be waiting for Wyatt to start making the calls. Once that happens, your part in all of this will be over and you ladies can return to your regularly scheduled lives, so to speak. Katie, don't expect to be getting any sleep tonight because as soon as the banquet is over, we'll pick you up and bring you to headquarters. Say around eleven-thirty?"

"Ladies, you may also want to carry one of these."

Stuart handed Katie and Melanie each a .45 caliber revolver.

"We have smaller guns, if you'd like a .22." Don said. "Meet me back here later this afternoon and I'll give you two some protection training. There's a practice range a few levels down."

Katie's mood suddenly became more focused. Her previous feeling of helplessness was replaced by one of total empowerment as she expertly loaded the weapon and aimed it toward the photo of Wyatt Gaynes on the screen.

"Don, I know how to use a .22, a .45, and several shotguns. I was born and raised in Minnesota, remember. We shoot duck, we shoot bear, we shoot elk, hell, we shoot fish."

"I'll keep that in mind," Stuart said.

Katie put the revolver into her purse.

"I'll get a holster for this later, but in the meantime, I have to get home and have a very long talk with my husband."

"You'd better make sure the safety is on that gun when you do." Melanie joked.

"C'mon, Katie, I'll walk you out," Stuart escorted Katie from the room.

"Well, I guess that leaves just you and me," Don said to Melanie after the others left. "Are you a sharp-shooter like your friend, or would you like me to give you some lessons?"

"Unlike my girlfriend," Melanie replied, "the only thing I learned how to shoot in the cold plains of Minnesota were shots of Tequila. Lead on Mr. Agent man."

Melanie followed Don into the hallway and tried to engage him in polite small talk.

"So, tell me, Don. What made you decide to become an UNCLE agent?"

"Would you believe...?

"Oh, please don't start that!"

"No, really. Would you believe it was because I hated my name?"

"Donald? What's wrong with Donald?"

"As in Duck?," He said with a grimace.

"Oh, now I get it."

"That's why I joined UNCLE I thought I would get a really cool spy name, like 007."

"So, Donald, what is your really cool spy name?"

"Don."

Again with that adorable smile, she thought.

"Don is a nice spy name, and a nice non-spy name, too. I think Mel is a great spy name. Think I'll keep it."

"Sounds good to me, too."

Melanie followed Don into the elevator which then descended another two floors. The door opened to a massive firing range.

"Don, this place is huge."

"You've only seen a small part, Mel. We have a full fitness room, swimming pool, sauna and spa. Sometimes when we're working on a serious operation, we can be here for days, sometimes weeks at a time, so we have to make it as comfortable for our agents as we can."

"Now I can see why you're single," she said.

"It's not that bad. You should try one of our Swedish massages," Don smiled. "Here we are. Let's start off with something small, like a .22."

Don showed Melanie how to hold the gun and position her body. She could feel the warmth of his breath on her neck, the strength of his taut muscles and something else pressing against her thigh she was pretty sure wasn't his gun.

As he held her arm, she aimed at the paper target and fired several shots. When Don brought the paper target to view her shot, he wasn't at all surprised to see that Melanie's shot had been right on target, exactly between the cut-out figure's legs.

"And here I thought you never fired a gun." Don said.

"Can I say that I was thinking of Wyatt when I pulled the trigger?"

"Well, the shot might not have exactly killed him, but it definitely would have turned him into a soprano."

They both laughed.

"I read the files about your, how do I put this, relationship?"

"More like relationshit," Melanie said. "I'd love to see what's in those files."

"Not much, really. We don't pay that much attention to personal affairs."

Don was beginning to feel uncomfortable discussing Melanie's assignment.

"So to speak," he tried a weak smile.

Cute, Melanie thought. He's embarrassed.

"I think you may have underestimated my abilities. Sure Wyatt and I have some history, but Don, that was a very long time ago. Whatever makes you think I can, how did you put it, distract him all night when I've not even seen him for more than twenty years?"

Don's eyes were peering deeply into Melanie's. He took his hand and gently brushed a piece of hair from her face.

"Melanie, I think you have no idea just how distracting you are."

He leaned down and gave her a soft, gentle, almost apprehensive kiss. At first she was going to protest, but Melanie was way beyond the age of sexual game-playing.

Don was amazingly strong, her body responded to his in a way she had never experienced with someone she had only just met. Maybe her failed marriages had injured her self-esteem, or the impending menopause was making her feel less than youthful, but it certainly felt wonderful to be reassured that she was still sexually attractive.

When she was finally able to catch her breath, she said, "So, Donald, Don, is there anything else you'd like to show me besides how to shoot and how to kiss?"

"Seems to me, you don't need any lessons from me on either of those skills. Don't be fooled by Wyatt's innocent demeanor, Mel. Remember, he's still the head of an international network of ruthless criminals who won't be as easily manipulated, not even by someone as talented as you."

Don had Melanie fire off a few more rounds towards a more conventional area of the paper card. While Don was extremely impressed by her shooting talent, he hoped that she would never have to use it on a moving target. He had seen too many agents who were overconfident on the firing range fall victim to someone else's more accurate aim.

Although the agency had loosened their policy on allowing women to become field agents, Don couldn't help feeling overly protective of the females with whom he partnered. He had purposely kept himself unavailable, some say even a bit cold, but not all of it was his choice. Sharon had been the one exception, and when word came from headquarters that she had been killed, his emotions were buried along with her.

It's not that he was without female companionship. That was one thing about the agency that the television show had depicted correctly. With his strong shoulders, high forehead, finely chiseled features, and unfortunate dimples, handsome would have been a good description, if it wasn't such a trite one when used to describe spies.

He was approaching an age where most men in his profession who were still breathing, were looking forward to retirement or a nice desk job. His hair was starting to show signs of gray, and he noticed it was thinning a bit more then he liked even though there was still quite a lot of it.

With his training and experience, he was quite surprised at his response to Melanie. Of course he had read the agency's file on her before they met, but it didn't tell him that she would have such a delightful sense of humor, a wonderful laugh, and the ability to distract him even when his mind was trying to focus on a very dangerous mission.

"Don, I think I've killed enough of these paper guys and it's almost ten-thirty. I told Wyatt I would call him, since he was so anxious for me to see his little stationery store, I think it would be a good idea to check out his place."

Remembering their assignment, Don found himself feeling a bit over-protective. He was also feeling unfamiliar pangs of jealousy.

"Look, Mel. I know we've asked you to help us with this mission, and you'll have plenty of back-up, but if you think it's too dangerous, I wouldn't hold anything against you if you decided not to go along."

"Don, you've already held a great deal against me," Melanie teased, "and I'm hoping that wasn't part of the training for what you're asking me to do with Wyatt."

"Mel, I..."

"Don't worry, Don. I'm a big girl, way over twenty-one. I'll be fine," She was rather enjoying Don's uncharacteristic loss of words. "I'll distract Wyatt, he won't know a thing. Besides, I owe him one. Actually, I owe him several, but one will do for now."

Don escorted Melanie from the bakery. He hoped she was as confident as she sounded. From the way she handled the gun, he had no doubt she could shoot. From the way she felt in his arms, he had no doubt she could kiss. As he watched her drive away to meet Wyatt, he also had no doubt that she could distract him long enough to help his team bring down the entire THRUSH organization.

And then some

Chapter Eleven

As Katie drove home, she didn't know how she was feeling. She was worried about James' health, and she was angry that he had been keeping his involvement with Wyatt from her. Throughout their marriage, she had never once kept any secrets from him and it was difficult for her to accept that he might not be the same man that she had married. Perhaps it was true what everyone had warned her about when he started his political career; power would corrupt even the most honest of men. Katie had the utmost faith in her husband that he would be the exception to the rule. Now she wasn't so sure.

The family home of State Senator James O'Brien wasn't much different from those of his constituents who lived on the lake on the outskirts of Abbeyville. Katie's wasn't sure if it was her nerves or the car driving over the designer brick and pebble driveway that was causing her hands to shake as she drove the pick-up into the three-car garage. Knowing what might await her when she entered the opulent house, Katie painfully reminisced the early years when the boys were toddlers and their home was a three-bedroom cottage. She began to wonder what else had changed beside their address.

After James won the Senate seat, he'd convinced Katie that they could afford to move into a bigger house. Prestige and political power was never an enticement for Kathleen Conner. Her small town roots were firmly embedded in the soil of Abbeyville, but she didn't put up too much of an argument when James showed her the two-story lakefront property which was to be their new home.

The exterior combination of sepia brick and stucco was both esthetically pleasing and environmentally functional. The stone pillars on the first floor gave the impression of a

Greek garden and the second floor was surrounded by a fenced-in wooden deck.

The house itself was a traditional two-story Midwestern style home; the first story was where the family entertained guests and ate family meals. James' home office was on the opposite side of the house. It had a separate entrance so he could meet his constituents and hold staff meetings without interrupting the rest of the family. It was his idea not to have traditional government offices in town because he didn't want the taxpayers footing the bill for rent on additional office space.

Upstairs, the master bedroom had a stone fireplace, walk-in closet and a full bath with a sunk-in tub and glass-enclosed shower with wall massage jets. Each of their sons had their own bedroom although they were smaller than the guest room, since they were only home during college breaks and summer vacation.

Katie opened the garage door, parked the truck inside and walked past the washer, dryer and furnace and up the stairs which led into the kitchen. She always felt a little bit guilty every time she past the dryer because she seldom used it, preferring nature's sunshine and wind to artificial gas heat. Fortunately the clothesline was well hidden between several ten foot pine trees in the backyard. It would be undignified for the neighbors to see their elected representative's tidy-whities blowing in the breeze. Now, as she made her way into the kitchen, Katie was wondering what other types of dirty laundry James might have been hiding from not only the neighbors, but his wife as well.

James was dressed and having coffee when Katie walked into the kitchen, baked goods in one hand, an excuse in the other. She felt like she had been caught by her parents sneaking into the house after staying out all night. It was amazing how something as mundane as a high school reunion could make adults nearly a half-century old feel like rebellious teenagers.

"I went to the bakery early and picked up those cinnamon buns you like."

She was hoping her voice didn't betray her. After all, it was partially true. However, as difficult as she knew it was going to be, she had to reveal the entire truth. She hoped her husband would do the same.

"Sweets from a sweetie. Thanks, Katie."

James gave his wife a kiss on the cheek and took the box from her.

"I just made some coffee. Doc said I have a clean bill of health and that little episode was only a fluke. This means I'll be fine to escort my beautiful wife to our reunion banquet and we can dance 'til midnight."

James put his arm around Katie's waist and gave her a little twirl. She felt so happy that he was healthy, she wanted to forget all about UNCLE, the mission and Wyatt Gaynes and just enjoy the moment, but she knew that wasn't possible. Katie needed to tell James what she knew and to also reassure him that, she loved him and would always support him no matter what happened in the future.

Katie released herself from James' embrace, poured herself a cup of coffee, took a deep breath and said the one line that struck fear in the hearts of married men, in any language in every part of the world;

"We need to talk."

Chapter Twelve

Across town, Melanie was staring at the card in her hand and wondered if she would have the courage to make the call. For some reason her heart was pounding and her palms were beginning to sweat. It was one thing feeling confident while she was leaning against Don's firm warm body, especially when that body was also holding a .45 caliber pistol, it was quite another standing in the bright sunshine all alone.

Her physiological response to Wyatt was completely illogical, and she had to force herself to ignore the danger signals her body was sending. Taking her cell phone from her purse, Melanie forced her trembling fingers to press the buttons that corresponded to the numbers written on Wyatt's business card. For a split second, she half-hoped he wouldn't answer. That second ended the moment she heard his voice say "Gaynes here".

"Wyatt? It's Melanie."

"Mel! What a nice surprise!"

Yes, I suppose you would think that.

"It really was nice to see you again," she lied, "and I thought I'd take you up on your offer to tour your place. Catch-up on, well ya know, things."

"I'd like that. You have the address, why don't you come right over. I'll cancel my appointments."

Melanie couldn't help notice that Wyatt sounded a bit too excited.

"That's really nice of you, Wyatt. I'll be right over."

"I'll be waiting."

Said the spider to the fly.

Standing outside Wyatt's quaint stationery store, Melanie was seriously beginning to think that everything Don and Stu had told her had been some fantastic practical joke. Living in a town where reality was only a sound stage and props could be manufactured at a moment's notice, Melanie couldn't help but wonder if the entire UNCLE scenario was some kind of elaborate prank at Katie and her expense. Although she had no idea why anyone would have gone through the trouble of creating such a scheme, or what their motivation would have been.

From what she could see, Wyatt's business was nothing more than exactly what it appeared to be. Rows of greeting cards were displayed on acrylic shelves that were supported by wires that were hung from the ceiling to the floor, so that a customer could see all of the merchandise from any location. Melanie was impressed with the warm, friendly ambiance, quite unlike what she knew of Wyatt's personality. The salesclerk was about to ask her if she could help her find something when Wyatt appeared from the back room.

"That's Ok, Janet. Mel is my guest," he said to his employee. "So, what do you think of Paper Passions?"

"Cute name, Wyatt," Melanie said. "Nice place, too. I see the print shop is right next door, how convenient."

Melanie did a quick eye scan of the area, trying to see something that would confirm Don's story, but she didn't notice anything even a bit suspicious. Putting aside her ulterior motive for the visit, Melanie turned her attention to the man who owned the store.

For a guy close to fifty, Wyatt was surprisingly fit and trim. He was only a few inches taller, although his legs were shorter, he made up for it with a very long, very taut torso. She was having more and more of a difficult time believing her old high school classmate, and one-time lover, was anything at all like the man Don and Stuart believed him to be.

"I'm so glad you called," Wyatt said, "but this is only the storefront. Let me give you the grand tour."

Wyatt held out his hand. Melanie cautiously took it, feeling an uncomfortable sensation when their fingers touched, she forced herself not to pull her hand away.

"I'd like that."

Melanie let Wyatt lead her through the store to the back office. Looking around, she noticed an ordinary desk, a computer, telephone and fax machine As far as she could tell, nothing that would indicate this was any different than any other business office. Melanie felt her breathing return to normal, then her defenses were suddenly raised as Wyatt led her into the storage room.

"C'mon, Wyatt. We don't need to hide in a closet to make out." She joked.

He responded to her statement with a laugh. "Mel, if I were going to make out with you, as you say, I'd take you in the back seat of my Mercedes."

"Oh, it's a Mercedes now, is it? I remember a red Chevy pick-up, back in the day."

"Oh, and what else do you remember from that day?"

Melanie was beginning to feel a bit uneasy, not about remembering Wyatt's truck, but the image of watching it speed away from her after he'd dropped her off at her parent's the night of the senior prom.

"Wyatt, let's not reminisce, too much ok? I'd really just like to see your store, and what's behind curtain number three."

"Ah, well, you've seen the store, it's not much more than this, but let me show you my hidden lair, so to speak."

Wyatt pulled the curtain back to reveal another door. Melanie was hoping he couldn't hear how hard her heart was beating. If Don's story was true she was about to enter the headquarters of THRUSH. Melanie followed Wyatt up the stairs. When Wyatt opened the door, she was relieved to find the stairs had led, not to a secret headquarters, but to an opulent apartment.

"You'll have to take off your shoes. The carpet is new and I don't want any of that Minnesota clay tracked in."

Melanie took off her shoes, thinking that Wyatt was really over doing the cleanliness obsession, but apparently that wasn't his only obsession. Wyatt's apartment looked like something out of Better Homes and Gardens. There was a huge glass wall that looked out over the lake and not a bit of dust to be seen. Even the kitchen was immaculate. What was missing, Melanie noticed, were any signs of a personal touch.

The walls were covered in beautiful art, but completely devoid of any photographs. The entire apartment looked as if it were a showroom, or a professionally staged movie set. At first glance it was certainly impressive, but upon a closer look, it was completely cold and impersonal, devoid of any sense that anyone actually lived there at all.

"This is amazing, Wyatt," Melanie stroked his ego. "I never would have expected such a beautiful apartment existed when the rest of the buildings on this street are all dilapidated storefronts."

"Well, I'll tell you a little secret. A few years ago this area was condemned by the city. There was an immediate revolt against their plans to take over the property using their power of Eminent Domain, which would have meant years of court battles. So, I suggested that they re-zone this area for mixed use. I had a little influence with a certain city councilman who helped push it through. He received all the credit for saving the town millions of dollars, and I was able to build this apartment."

Melanie felt a little warning shiver go up her back when Wyatt mentioned the councilman. She didn't want to ask, but she needed to know.

"That councilman didn't happen to be James O'Brien?"

"Yes, as a matter of fact it was. James and I go way back, as you know. I helped with his campaigns for city council and recently state Senate, so he did me a little favor. That's how these things work in a small town."

"And in a big city, too, from what little I know about politics."

Melanie didn't know that much about politics at all, but she did know it wasn't that big of a leap from influencing a local city zoning change to influencing a State legislation bill. As much as she didn't want to believe what the agents had showed her, it was becoming more and more evident that her former classmates all had some kind of connection to Wyatt, even her best friend's husband.

"I hate to cut this short, Mel, but I have some business to take care of. Will I see you later at the reunion banquet?"

At last, she thought, with a bit of luck and some good acting, now was the perfect time to make her move. She wrapped her arms around Wyatt's neck and kissed him, gently at first, then with greater intensity. His reaction was electric and immediate, and Melanie was completely enjoying every inch of it.

"I know. You have a meeting," she faked a seductive whisper. "Why don't we pick this up later tonight after the party?"

"Definitely," Wyatt grinned. "If you were impressed with the living room, I can't wait to show you my master bedroom."

Wyatt opened a door at the far side of the room.

"Take the back stairs, they lead directly to the street. See you tonight."

After leaving Wyatt's Melanie got into her car and was about to phone Don with her report that she hadn't seen anything suspicious when she glanced in her rear view mirror and saw Charles walking toward the alley behind Wyatt's store. His was so intent on where he was walking, he was totally oblivious to anything going on around him.

Melanie knew she had to make a decision in a matter of seconds. Her mission was to find out what Wyatt was planning. She knew that Charles was part of the plan. She also knew that this was her best opportunity to find out exactly what that plan was, and she also knew that Don would never be able to get here in time.

Melanie replayed every episode of the entire four year season of the sixties television show in her mind and made a decision. She would get inside, get the information, and if she were caught, could act out any number of memorized scripted dialogues to get herself out.

Just as she had been instructed, Melanie triggered the communicator pen and tracking device Don had given her to be sure they were active. She checked to make certain the gun was positioned securely in her purse, then she followed Charles into the alley and through the rear entrance. She was so quiet, he never once looked behind him.

Taking slow, quiet steps, Melanie continued to follow him through a darkened hallway. Charles stopped in front of a blank wall where she saw him press a switch and the entire wall slid open, revealing an immense room and a huge world map suspended from the ceiling. From her position, Melanie could see the entire operation. When Wyatt came in from the other entrance, she instinctively looked around her hiding place to make sure there were no security cameras anywhere nearby.

Either Wyatt was overly confident or just ignorant because she had no problem seeing and hearing everything that was going on from where she was standing. At least she could report back to Don how to break into Wyatt's operation, she thought. She hoped that would be enough.

Melanie wanted to leave, but she knew she needed to stay, more to satisfy her own curiosity then to complete an assignment. What she overheard made her wish she'd headed her instincts to run.

Wyatt walked in front of the map and addressed the forty or so men who were seated at their computer stations,

Melanie was not surprised that there weren't any women. Charles was standing next to Wyatt, looking very anxious, even with Wyatt's arm reassuringly positioned on his shoulder. There was an uneasy silence as those in attendance waited in eager anticipation for their leader to address them.

"Gentlemen," Wyatt began, "We have all worked very hard for this day. First, let me congratulate Chuck here, our computer genius, who worked tirelessly to help make this happen."

There was some polite applause. Melanie could sense that those in the room didn't quite share Wyatt's admiration.

"Thanks, Wyatt," Chuck began, "but that's not really..."

Wyatt cut him off before he had a chance to complete his sentence.

"Tomorrow, I'll be meeting with our chief operatives from sixteen countries. Once they see how well everything is working, and it is working very well I might add, each of you will receive a password to your Swiss bank account and the bonus I promised you of one million dollars."

A huge cheer went up from the crowd. Then, a voice came from the back which confirmed to Melanie that everything Don and Stuart told her was the absolute truth.

"Hey, Wyatt. Those one million dollars had better not be from your presses!"

The sound of the men's rambunctious celebration followed Melanie's every step as she ran from the building and continued to haunt her all the way to her car.

Wyatt's evil laugh stayed with her much longer.

Chapter Thirteen

Checking her rear view mirror to be sure she wasn't being followed, Melanie nearly ran into a parked car as she sped back to the bakery and UNCLE headquarters. After showing the salesclerk her badge, she was escorted once again to the rear of the bakery. Minutes later, she was in Don's office, surprised to see Katie sitting there.

"Don was right," both women said in unison.

"Of course I was, ladies. I'm always right."

Melanie couldn't help notice that Don had flashed her a slight grin.

"Katie just returned also," Stuart said. "She said she has something to show us.".

Katie opened her purse and placed a pile of papers on the consol.

"James gave me these finance reports that he got from his so-called best friend. He confessed everything. After Wyatt became James' campaign manager, apparently he started doing a bang-up job of fund raising. At the time, we thought the contributions were coming from the Gaynes' business contacts, and fund-raising events, but after James was elected, Wyatt showed him these."

Katie handed two stacks of papers to Don. The covers on both reports were identical and were dated back to when James had first launched his senate campaign. Both covers were also signed by Wyatt Gaynes.

"It appears that Wyatt was filing falsified reports with the elections board to cover these campaign contributions."

"And James didn't know anything about this?"

"No, Don. My husband did not know anything about this!"

"Relax, Katie. I believe you. Besides, if James was trying to cover up his involvement, he wouldn't have given you these files."

"Tell me, Don. How much trouble is he in?"

The worry in Katie's voice was obvious.

"Katie, as I told you, UNCLE isn't involved in State government affairs. We deal with matters on a much larger international scale. Not that Minnesota state politics isn't important, but it's just not something we get involved in."

"Well, Mr. big shot UNCLE agent, how about what I just overheard at Wyatt's place?" Melanie said. "By the way, if I could get into that hidden room so easily, how come you couldn't?"

Don leaned back in his chair and loosened his tie before he replied.

"Melanie, real life law enforcement is a lot more complicated than what you see on television. We can't just go busting through doors, guns blazing. We still have to follow certain procedures, like getting a search warrant, but it seems that Wyatt has all the judges in the entire county in his back pocket, so by the time the warrants arrived, Wyatt would clear out all the evidence."

"Seems to me you guys can't do anything at all, which is why you're using us, right?"

Melanie was feeling her anger and frustration begin to come to the surface.

"Mel, these guys asked us to help them, remember?" Katie argued. "They're not using us, and after the way Wyatt's treated James, I have no reservations about this mission, and neither should you."

Katie paused a moment to look at her watch.

"Don, it's getting close to two, and I have to get to the hotel, meet the band, and finish the decorations before four so I'll have time to go home and change."

"Don't worry about tonight. Wyatt Gaynes messed with the wrong Senator and he definitely should not have messed with the Senator's wife. I'll see you later."

As Melanie watched her friend leave the room, she couldn't help by feel impressed by Katie's determination and unwavering faith in her beliefs about right and wrong, even to the point of putting herself at risk to protect those she loved. She was almost jealous of Katie's solid married life, when hers had been a series of failed relationships.

"She's really something, isn't she?" Don said to Melanie.

"You're just figuring that out now? As far back as elementary school and long past graduation, Katie has been my rock. I can't begin to tell you how many hours of telephone time we burned over the years."

"You know, from reading your files, I would have thought it would have been the reverse. Do you want to get out of here and grab a late lunch?"

Melanie didn't know if Don was asking her out, or just being polite. Being in the acting profession, she could usually tell when someone was playing a role, or disguising a hidden agenda. There was a distinct look in the eye, a body movement that didn't quite match the words, but she didn't see any hidden messages coming from Don. Either he was a very good liar, or just a very good man. It took a great deal for Melanie to trust anyone and the jury was still out on Don.

"I've been going on that breakfast muffin and coffee, so something more substantial sounds great. You buying?" It didn't hurt to ask, She thought.

"I'll put it on my expense account. There's a great diner a few blocks from here. We can walk, if you'd like."

"Walk? I'm from L.A. What's walk?"

For a few moments, Melanie allowed her natural defenses to relax as she and Don made their way to the diner. She was very conscious of his strong, solid strides and how easily she was able to match his steps. Although she was looking straight ahead, she could feel him glancing at her every so often. Whether it was her overactive imagination or a bit of feminine ego, she was definitely enjoying the attention, imagined or not.

When they arrived at the restaurant, Don opened the door for Melanie then followed her to a corner booth. The waitress handed them each a menu.

"Hey, Don. I think this is the first time I've seen you with a date. Do you want your usual? Burger, plain with a pickle on the side?"

"She's not..." he began then, after he looked at Melanie, didn't finish the sentence. "That'll be fine, Kim."

"Sounds good to me, also," Melanie replied, ignoring the waitress's comment completely. "Out in L.A. they toss a complete salad between the bun and they call it health food. Kim, could you please throw in some unhealthy fries with that? Thanks."

"So, you're not a California vegetarian?"

Melanie could feel her face flush from Don's warm smile. Always the observant agent, Don was pleased to see her reaction. Like the waitress said, it had been a very long time since there was another body, especially a female one, sharing a booth, let alone anything else, with him.

"No way, Don. You know I'm from the heartland of beef. I'll take a good burger or steak over tofu any day. The fries were just a small indulgence."

It was becoming more apparent to Melanie that their little lunch was turning into something a bit more interesting, and she was beginning to enjoy it, even more than the giant beef patty the waitress put on the table. To avoid any mistake in her theory, Melanie redirected the conversation back to a more comfortable direction.

"So, Mr. Agent man, what exactly is the plan?"

"Well, for one thing, you've got to stop calling me Mr. Agent man. I'm just a bartender, remember?"

"And the locals all believe that, I'm sure. With all the places in the world you could have landed, how did you end up in Abbeyville?"

"That's just it, Mel. I've been all over the world and found I liked small towns, so when this assignment was offered, I took it. Besides, they make the very best hamburgers." he said as the waitress put their plates on the table. "But there is something to be said about large cities, too. To be honest, I miss the theaters of New York, the night life in Paris. I even miss the traffic of the Los Angeles freeways."

Melanie took a bite of her burger. She had to admit, Don was right about the food, but she totally disagreed with him about the L.A. traffic.

"Ok, now I know you're lying. No one misses rush hour on the 405."

For some reason, Melanie felt nervous. She tried to tell herself it was because of what she had just seen at Wyatt's, or that Don and Stuart were planning something she was going to be involved with, or maybe it was the fact that Don had the most piecing baby-blue-eyes she had ever seen that weren't created by artificial colored contacts.

"Mel, would you answer a question that wasn't in your files?"

"Yes, they're real," she replied with a grin.

She was pleased to see that this time it was Don's face that was turning red.

"Well, to be totally candid, that intel, uh, was in your files," he stammered. "Along with the fact that that's not exactly your natural hair color."

"Ok, Don, now you're getting personal," She faked annoyance.

The truth was, Melanie was glad that Don knew details of her life. First dates were awkward enough having to answer a lot of personal questions and make small talk. It was a nice change not to have to jump through those usual hoops, even though she wished she had the same access to Don's information as well.

"I was just wondering why a beautiful, talented, and successful woman has remained an elusive single lady?"

"You mean me?" Melanie replied.

"No. The waitress. Of course I mean you. Our agency knows about your former manager Paul and your divorces with Abe and Frank..."

"That's enough of the list of Whose Who that have been in my, well let's just say my life, Don. I'll be the first to admit my track record hasn't been all that great, but it's a bit more complicated," she said. "When you're an actor, you're constantly pretending to be someone else, and so are the men who are your co-stars. It can become very confusing, especially when you're in a romantic role. If you're good at playing the part believably, that your character is in love with the character that your co-star is playing, but you, the real you, isn't in love with that other person. After a few months of a production, it can be difficult to return to reality once the scene is over. Sometimes the lines become blurred, which can lead to a lot of complications."

"I can understand that. Many times I've had to play different roles when I was on an undercover assignment. But then again, I was the only one pretending," Don said.

"But the difference is that when your assignment is over, only one of you knows you were acting. The problem for me was that I fell in love with the character Abe was playing, and I suppose he fell in love with the character I was playing, but none of it was real."

"So, what you're saying is that when a man says he loves you, you're not certain if he's being sincere, or just playing a part?"

"No, what I'm saying is that sometimes I'm not sure if what I'm saying is what I'm really feeling. If those hugs and kisses are from me, Melanie Tyler, or from the fantasy character I'm pretending to be. That's the beauty of voice-over acting. The only thing that's not real is my voice, I don't have to pretend to enjoy kissing someone, or confuse who the other voice actors are," She smiled.

Damn, this was really beginning to feel like a date, she thought. Now it just feels like another audition.

"I never really thought about actors in quite that way," he said. "For me, I think the hardest role I've ever had to play as an UNCLE agent was to try and fit into a small town in Minnesota."

"I can certainly understand that," Melanie took a bite of her hamburger.

"It took me awhile to figure out that when someone offered me a hot dish they weren't trying to set me up with their sister."

Melanie started to laugh and nearly spit out her food.

"When I first got here, I was in the bakery and the ladies were talking about going to the lake for the weekend. I made the fatal mistake of asking which lake, and you should have seen the look on their faces."

"Yes, I can see where you would need an interpreter, at least for the first few weeks," Melanie said. "So, I guess we have something in common. We've both played fictional roles and tried to fit into an environment that was completely foreign to us, but we adapted."

"Yes, I suppose you can say that, but right now this diner feels pretty familiar and you're not playing a role," Don said.

"Except secret agent M9." Melanie added.

"Yes, except for M9," Don smiled, "and I'm not undercover...yet," his smile got wider, "so if I kiss you now, you'll know that it's because I want to, not because I'm on assignment pretending to be someone who wants to, and you'll know it's real."

That last sentence was the first personal statement Don had made to a woman in a very long time and it both surprised and frightened him at the same time. After he had been assigned the mission, Don had read through the files of all the agent and non-agent operatives. The details of Melanie's relationship with Wyatt Gaynes was something the agency needed to use if their plan was to succeed, but the more time he spent with the lady from L.A., the more uncomfortable he was feeling about putting her into what could turn out to be a very compromising position. In actuality he didn't want Melanie any where near Wyatt Gaynes. It was a feeling that was very uncharacteristic for a spy, much less one who had been working in the field for more than twenty years.

Don was in his first year of med school, majoring in forensic pathology when he was first recruited into the Agency, he had been excited and flattered to have been chosen to serve his country. They warned him of the lonely lifestyle, or that he might never have a serious relationship, and at twenty-five, it didn't seem to matter. He was enjoying his work, the travel, and especially the women. Then, almost over night, he was looking at his life from the other side of the hill, and the view was pretty barren.

When UNCLE had initially formed, the mandatory retirement age for an agent had been set at forty, but that was changed in the mid-eighties when the Agency realized they were losing some of their best and most experienced agents due to an outdated policy. Now as long as agents could pass their annual exams and physicals, they could stay in the field until they either decided to retire, or an enemy agent retired them. After women began to be recruited as field agents, the ban against inter-agency marriage was also ended. Don wasn't one to stay in one place long enough to form any serious relationships, and after losing one female partner six years ago, he was quite content to be a loner. But now the many years alone were starting to feel like many lonely years. The more time he spent in a small town added to his angst. Watching the townspeople, parents, and sometimes grandparents his own age going to picnics, playing baseball and soccer, he wondered if it had been worth the trade.

Then he and his team completed an important assignment and he was reminded that his job was to make the world a safer place for those parents and grandparents and all those kids. He knew he wouldn't have traded his life for any one of theirs. Still, it would be nice to someday have a place to call home and maybe a woman to share that home with. Or maybe a dog.

Melanie's voice brought Don's attention back to the present.

"Well, I can't be sure until you do."

"Do what?" he said, faking a memory loss.

"Kiss me for real."

"When this is all over, I plan on doing exactly that. I also plan on not stopping with only one kiss, just so you know."

Melanie glanced around at the other diners to see if any of them had noticed the air conditioner in the diner had suddenly stopped working. In a matter of seconds it became very obvious to her that she was the only one in the place who was sweating.

Trying to remain nonchalant and failing miserably, she replied, "I'm leaving Monday morning, so I'm not really sure how much time we'll have when this is all over."

Melanie forced the last bite of French fry down her throat, then motioned to the waitress that she would like a refill of her coffee. She was actually quite full of caffeine, but she needed an excuse to make the lunch break last a bit longer. She didn't want the date, if this was a date, to end.

Twenty-four hours was no where near enough time to get to know someone, she thought, let alone feel as if they'd known each other all their lives. During her acting career Melanie had read enough B-movie scripts to know the "love at first sight" scenario never ended well, but as Don had pointed out earlier, happy endings depicted in fictional movies or television, are very seldom the way real life turns out.

While she could tell herself all the logical reasons why she shouldn't be having feelings for the tall, dark, and handsome, spy guy, all logic went out the window when the illogical heart burst through the front door. The one thing that both her logical mind and her illogical body were in complete agreement was the fact that she wanted, more than anything, to spend whatever free time she had in Abbeyville with Don. The more time she spent with him, the less enthusiastic she was becoming about her impending assignment with Wyatt.

"We'll have plenty of time after we complete the mission. You have the capsule, just in case. The agency isn't about compromising anyone's morals."

"It's nice to know you agent guys care about the morals of us gals."

"This agent guy is only interested in one gal at the moment, and her morals have nothing to do with it." Don's warm smile said a great deal more than his words.

Before Melanie had a chance to respond, the waitress came to the table with their bill. Not assuming anything, she placed the paper between them. Melanie moved to pick it up, but Don beat her to it.

"What's my half?" She asked.

"Nothing. I'll take care of this. Remember, I said I have an expense account."

"I can take care of my own bill," Melanie replied taking a twenty from her wallet.

"Let's compromise. You leave the tip this time, and we'll switch next time." Don said.

He rose from his seat and began walking toward the cash register before she had a chance to argue.

"Next time? Who said anything about there being a next time?"

Melanie said aloud to an empty chair. She still wasn't sure if this had been an official first date, but she was very sure that, in spite of his trying to hide the fact, Don had revealed he had feelings for her. But for now, exploring those feelings further would have to wait. In a few hours, she was going to have to cheat on her possible new boyfriend while pretending to seduce her very old ex-boyfriend.

For an actress who was quickly approaching the big five-0, it didn't get any better than this

.

Chapter Fourteen

Katie was just finishing putting the last photo of the class of 1972 on the display board when Stuart entered the ballroom.

"Katie, this place looks fantastic. You really did a wonderful job."

"Thanks, Stu. I heard there were about ten more people who checked into the hotel this morning, so that brings the total close to one-hundred and fifty, with guests. I guess high school reunions aren't so old fashioned as everyone seems to think. I'm almost finished and was just on my way home."

"Then I'm glad I got here when I did. I need to take you back to headquarters for about an hour to go over the final details of what we're going to be doing tonight."

"Now?" Katie said. "It's already four o'clock, Stu. I was going to sit in a hot tub for an hour before this craziness begins, and I'm not talking about your plan, or Wyatt's either which are both pretty crazy."

Katie gave the room one last visual inspection, then, reluctantly, followed Stuart to his car. Even though he had told her that she wouldn't be in any real danger, there was a huge difference between playing spies and being a real spy. But she would do whatever she could to protect her family and the man she loved.

When Katie questioned James about the UNCLE accusations, he had gone painfully silent. Over the years, she had seen sadness, love, hope, joy and a wide variety of emotions in the bright green eyes of her Irish-American husband, but in all that time she had never seen shame.

James didn't even try to deny what Katie told him about what the UNCLE agents had said. He told her that at first Wyatt had only asked for a few harmless favors. He thought Wyatt's idea to cancel the city's plan to condemn the blighted downtown area and change the zoning ordinance was a good one. Everyone else on the council thought James' idea was innovative, and it did result in bringing more commerce to the business community. Wyatt never once tried to take credit, but he also never let James forget whose idea it actually had been.

A few years later, Wyatt needed to add a sub-basement beneath his store and he asked James to fast-track the permits. James didn't see any harm in asking a favor from the Planning Commissioner, who didn't see any harm in granting it. That was the last time Wyatt had asked James for any special treatment. Then, saying he wanted to return the favor, Wyatt offered to manage James' senate campaign. James' gut instincts were sending warning signals throughout the campaign, but he chose to ignore them. The thought of being able to help so many Minnesota residents as a state senator, and perhaps someday at the national level as a congressman, drowned out the warning noise of doubt and suspicion, until he could no longer hear them.

James had told Katie everything, including the details of the secret meeting he and Wyatt had back in December. A group of crazy Green fanatics were petitioning the state to ban a certain dye which had been shown to be highly toxic if released into the water system. James had read the reports, and listened to the ecologists and other scientists who had come to the state capital in support of the ban.

At first, James had agreed with the findings and was in the process of adding his name to the bill when he'd received a phone call from Wyatt. That's when James found out about the second set of finance statements and Wyatt's demand that he would release them to the elections board unless James not only didn't co-sponsor the bill, but worked very hard to make sure that particular dye would not be on the toxic chemical list. When James had asked him why that particular dye, Wyatt had only said that it was something he needed in his print shop and that was the only answer he was going to get.

James had agonized over the vote for months, with Wyatt calling him nearly every day. Although Wyatt kept reassuring him that the dye was harmless, James suspected there was something more to it than Wyatt was letting on, but he didn't have a choice. He called in several favors and made additional promises to sway the other senators to vote against the ban, and when it came down to a tie, it was James that had cast the deciding vote. Right before he'd collapsed on the Senate floor.

Being a good Catholic, James went to confession nearly every Sunday, but revealing all of this to his wife was the hardest confession he had ever made. He didn't think there were enough Our Fathers or Hail Marys that would absolve him.

Katie had listened. She cried. She hugged James and, of course, she'd forgiven him, but her original plan to ask James for his permission to join the UNCLE team went out the window. Instead, she uncharacteristically told James that, after the reunion banquet, she wasn't coming home until Sunday morning. James started to protest, fearing his wife was putting herself in danger, but he could tell by the determination in her eyes that Katie's mind was made up. If there was anything James had learned over the years, was that while his wife could debate with the best of them, when she'd made up her mind, the argument was over.

Katie relayed an abbreviated version of the story to Stuart as they drove to the bakery, and walked through the entrance once again.

"In all the years I've lived in Abbeyville, I don't think I've ever been in this place as much as I have today. I do my own baking, don't cha know." Katie said.

"No, I don't believe that detail was in your file," Stuart smiled. "This location is hard on us agents, too. I can't tell you how many pounds I've put on since I was transferred back here. Those fresh donuts in the morning are addictive. Here we are Katie."

Stuart pulled the car in front of the entrance to the bakery. Another man in a suit opened the car door for her and she followed him and Stuart into the bakery.

"This is Agent Carl." Stuart made the introductions. "He'll fill you in on the details of what you'll be doing tonight. I'm going to find with Don, and we'll meet you later."

Stuart walked down one of the many hallways in the underground headquarters while Carl pointed Katie in the opposite direction.

"I've heard a great deal about you, Mrs. O'Brien," Carl said, "I know you're pretty up to date on most of new computers on the market, so what I'm about to show you might seem a bit strange."

"Oh, like a secret UNCLE headquarters underneath a bakery isn't strange?" she said.

"I know what you mean. Anyway, this is the mainframe of the Midwest operation. What you'll be doing tonight is connecting our system with Wyatt's so we can monitor everything that he's doing."

Carl switched on the lights and instantly Katie felt as if she had been transported back in time. On each computer station sat a Radio Shack TRS-80.

"Carl, you have got to be kidding me. This is the twenty-first century, why on earth would you be using such dinosaurs?"

"It's very simple, Katie. All the hackers use such advanced computer language now, forty year old tech is so out of date it's pretty much hack-proof. Hardly anyone programs in Basic or TRSDOS because it's so old."

"Does this ever take me back," Katie said. "When I was twenty-four, James bought me a Commodore PET for Christmas. I don't think I moved from that thing until two weeks past New Year."

"And we're still using those, too, but for what you'll be doing later, this is all you'll need."

"And what exactly will I be doing?" Katie asked.

"Now that we know exactly how to get into Wyatt's headquarters, thanks to Melanie's surveillance, we're going to break in and plant the transmitting devices. You'll be sitting here in this room transferring the information as it comes in. We need to know what he's planning for tomorrow and to do that, we need his phone lines re-directed to ours before he starts making those calls."

Katie was very skeptical. Of course she knew Basic computer language and she was also well versed in more modern programming, as a hobby more than anything else. She didn't think what Carl was asking her to do would be that difficult, provided the guys on the other end did their part. Of that she wasn't quite as certain.

What she was certain of however, was that she had less than two hours to get ready for the reunion banquet and she needed a ride back to the hotel to get her car. Fortunately, Melanie was waiting for her outside the bakery.

"Stuart called and asked me to come pick you up. Are you ready for all of this?"

"If you mean the reunion, yes, everything is ready. If you mean this insanity with Wyatt and the rest of this undercover spy stuff, I have no idea. What about you?"

"To tell you the truth, I'm having a great deal of fun, especially with Don. I trust the real agents know what they're doing, so I'm not worried. How are you doing?"

"I'm running on pure adrenalin, but other than that I agree with you. James isn't too happy about it, but I assured him his wife can handle a lot more than planning fund raisers and baking pies."

"Of that, I have no doubt," Melanie said.

Melanie parked her car next to Katie's truck.

"Thanks. Hey, I really have to get home, try and take a quick nap, and get ready for tonight. See you later."

As Katie drove away, Melanie walked back to the hotel with a great deal on her mind. She knew she needed to focus on the plan for the long evening ahead with the supposed criminal mind Wyatt, but her thoughts kept drifting toward a certain bartender slash UNCLE agent named Donald.

Chapter Fifteen

When Melanie returned to her hotel room, she took a very long bath and an even longer nap. The two-hour time difference was beginning to catch up with her and she knew she wasn't going to be getting much sleep the next 48 hours. In the back of her mind, she was hoping there would be time for her to share some of those hours with Don.

Melanie had packed an exquisite black and white Dior gown which accentuated her well-toned curves and created just the right amount of cleavage to be classified as elegant, sensual, and a little bit dangerous. Although she hadn't planned on making a Hollywood style entrance at the banquet, she was now officially on the hunt and wanted to make sure she was well armed.

She was fairly certain that Wyatt wouldn't have cared what she was wearing as long as she offered to have him remove it. She also knew that his ego would be a great deal more inflated if he were seen with a classy woman wearing an expensive designer dress and a bit of bling. It was times like these when Melanie could appreciate her career. In her heart, she was still a mid-westerner and material things were never that important to her, but she had to admit a certain amount of personal satisfaction that she could walk into any store on Rodeo Drive and pay cash for whatever she wanted to buy.

After the cast's last contract negotiations were finalized Melanie's salary was raised to six figures an episode with a guarantee season of twenty-two. Her biggest expense was her condominium on Ocean Avenue in Santa Monica. Unlike her co-stars, who were native Californians, Melanie never tired of watching the sunset over the Pacific Ocean from her balcony.

It had taken all of her best acting skills to pretend to be impressed when Wyatt had given her a tour of his apartment. She wasn't looking forward to using those same talents, later that night, to pretend to be impressed by him. Melanie also knew that if she were getting ready for a night with Don, she would not have had to fake her excitement.

Don had assured her that she wouldn't be in any real danger, but just in case, the former Girl Scout was going to be well prepared. She checked the safety on the gun before putting it, the cigarette case, communicator pen, and the capsule Don had given her, into her purse. Over the years she had been cast in small bit roles on many crime dramas and had even been the dead body on three episodes of Law and Order. The actress in her was more than ready to improvise an unscripted scene. It was a good thing the hotel doesn't have metal detectors, she thought, as she made her way to the elevator.

When she arrived at the lobby, Melanie couldn't help but be impressed at how beautiful the banquet hall had become. The casual ambiance of the previous evening had been totally transformed into a much more formal affair. The men were in suits, some were even wearing tuxedos and the women were dressed to the nines. The one thing that they all had in common was how much they had all aged. For a split second Melanie thought she was looking at the parents of her classmates and it took her another second to realize the faces she was seeing actually belonged to her peers.

Walking past the outer bar, Melanie caught Don giving her the full body once-over. She was quite pleased by his reaction, but once she spotted Wyatt at the reception table, her attention was completely focused on him. She walked up behind him and placed her hand softly on his shoulder. In her in her most alluring, seductive voice, she said,

"What table are you sitting at, Wyatt?"

Wyatt was a bit startled, but regained his composure the moment he saw whose hand was touching him.

"I'm at table sex." he said picking up his card. "I mean six."

Melanie cringed at Wyatt's attempt at crude humor, but went along with it. She reached to pick up her card, purposely leaning into Wyatt's side and brushing against his shoulder.

"Oh look, I'm at table sex, too."

She faked surprise since Katie had arranged all the table assignments, Melanie already knew that she and Wyatt were at the same table. Wyatt's smile reminded Melanie of a cobra who was just about to strike.

"How about you buy me a drink and I'll meet you at our table?" Melanie's emphasis of the word our was designed to send the message to Wyatt that it didn't matter who else was sitting with them, they owned the entire table. If there was one thing that Melanie knew how to do was use her voice to communicate subtle messages that the listener didn't even know they were hearing, but were very well understood.

"Absolutely!" Wyatt replied, a bit too eagerly, "But it's an open bar, so I won't really be buying you a drink. Would you like a White Russian to go with that beautiful black and white dress you're wearing?"

Melanie faked a small laugh. "Nice of you to notice, Wyatt, but I think I'd rather have a glass of wine. Anything white would be fine, thank you."

Melanie gave Wyatt a light kiss on his cheek and began walking towards table six. On the way, she spotted Katie and James sitting at table number one. As she began to walk over to say hello, James rose from his chair and walked away.

"What's up with James?" Melanie said to Katie."Was it something I said?"

"No, he's still feeling embarrassed about the fact we know what he did with Wyatt. He almost didn't come tonight, but I told him that I needed him here, so he can make excuses to everyone when I have to leave early."

"Well, please tell him that I don't blame him for anything. He was just another victim of Wyatt's scheming ways," Melanie lowered her voice to just above a whisper and added, "How does he feel about you working with UNCLE?"

"To be honest, I don't really care how he feels. I didn't want to tell the agents, but James and I really got into it last night. When I told him I was going to work with the agency, he said that this was his mess and he should be the one to fix it, not his wife."

"You're kidding? Did he really say that? What is it with men that they feel they have to protect us weak little women?"

"Maybe because they never grew out of the caveman mentality," Katie added. "Look over there, even Stu seems to have assumed the role, gay or not."

Melanie pointed to Stuart who was standing on the opposite side of the room watching over Katie and Melanie like a mother hen.

"Give me a break!" Katie said. "Where's Wyatt, by the way?"

"I'm not sure."

Melanie scanned the room to see if Wyatt had made it back to their table, but his chair was empty.

"I'm supposed to meet him at our table, but he's not back yet. Don't worry, Katie. With any luck, after tonight, you'll be back to being Mrs. James O'Brien, wife and mother and you can leave all the fix'n to the man."

"Here's hoping. I'll be up all night re-programming Wyatt's computer, but right now I'm just going to relax and try to have a good time, like the normal guests."

Katie was pleased to see how many couples were on the dance floor.

"Everyone seems to be enjoying the band. That's a good start." Melanie reassured her. "There's Wyatt. He's talking to Chuck by the balcony door."

"You call that talking? Chuck looks like he's about to take a swing at him. Oh, look at who just joined them, and he doesn't look all that happy either."

Melanie was watching the scene between Wyatt, Charles, and Eric when the three men moved outside. She looked across the room and noticed Stuart was gone.

"You stay here and wait for James, Katie. I'm going outside and try to hear what they're saying."

"Ok, be careful."

Melanie opened her purse, removed the cigarette case and turned on the communicator. The antenna was ultra-sensitive and could pick up conversations from a much longer distance than her own ears. She knew that Don would be able to hear everything that was being transmitted through the case. Pretending not to notice the men, Melanie walked over to a bench at the far end of the balcony, lit her cigarette and listened to the whispered, heated argument which was going on behind her. She recognized Charles'whiney voice immediately.

"Wyatt, I want out. I heard what you told the staff and we both know you're lying. I want no part of this."

Wyatt's tone was a great deal calmer and a great deal colder.

"It's a bit late to get cold feet now, don't you think Chuck? You took my money and now you want to back out? I don't think that's fair, do you, Eric?"

"Wyatt, I've done all I can for you and I agree with Chuck. This ends now!"

Eric's words sounded strong, but Melanie's professionally trained ear could tell, he didn't believe a word of what he was saying. She also knew by Wyatt's tone that he believed every word that was carefully, and threateningly, coming from his lips.

"Now, now guys. You know I can't let you do that. Not when I'm so close to putting this entire deal together, but I promise you that once the operation is successfully completed our relationship will be over. The truth is, your value to me is finished and after tomorrow night, I seriously doubt the two of you will be seeing me again."

There was a moment of dead silence and Melanie thought there might be something wrong with her listening device. She felt the implication in Wyatt's veiled threat, and wondered if he meant that no one else would be seeing Eric or Charles ever again either.

The transmission continued with Wyatt's light-hearted voice, "And speaking of relationships, I have another one I'm much more interested in at the moment with a very gorgeous lady who is waiting for me at our table and I don't want her thinking I ditched her again."

Melanie closed the cigarette case and quickly headed through the far door so she could get to the table before Wyatt. She made it to her seat just as he arrived with her wine.

"They only had some house brand Chardonnay. This isn't exactly Napa Valley."

Wyatt sat next to Melanie who thanked him for the drink by positioning her thigh next to his. Although she had never starred in a feature film, Melanie was certain she would have received an Oscar for the performance she was about to give.

More of their classmates began arriving and the rest of the seats at their table filled. Melanie and Wyatt spent the dinner part of the evening talking with their former classmates. Wyatt did his best to pretend interest in anyone who tried to get in a word of conversation. He responded to their praise of his brother's success by talking incessantly about his own accomplishments.

It was a shame that his father died and left control of the paper mill to his brother but what a fantastic business his stationery and print store was, he bragged. Yes, it was quite devastating when his fiancée Brenda left him to marry his brother, but he loved the freedom of the single life.

And on it went.

After listening to Wyatt's unabridged and highly inflated autobiography for the umpteenth time, Melanie excused herself to go to the ladies' room where she met Katie.

"So, how is it going with Mr. Silver?" Katie asked.

"He's as smooth as silver, as they say and just as tarnished. I'm just glad Don gave me protection and I don't mean the latex kind!"

"I don't envy you, Melanie. All I have to do is hack into some computer systems, you have to hack into that slime ball, and pretend to like it."

"If you knew how many jerks I had to pretend to like before I broke into the voice-over business, it would make your skin crawl. I know it did mine at the time. I'm really getting my money's worth from all those acting classes, I can tell you that."

"Mel, do you really think you can convince Wyatt that you're still in love with him? I know you're a good actress but really, can you pull this off?"

"Katie, you know that Wyatt and I have a history and while it's certainly not true today, once upon a time, I had genuine feelings for him, but that was a very long time ago and I was a very different person. But I doubt Wyatt sees it that way. I'm counting on his over-inflated ego to make him believe the fantasy of a girl with a high school crush pining for him all these years."

"You sure that's all it is? A fantasy?"

"Ok, I'll admit that when I first saw Wyatt last night by the lake, I could feel my body react to him, and I was rather surprised, but I think it was just the last embers of a dying flame, one that was permanently extinguished by what we've learned about the real Wyatt Gaynes. From what I heard, and especially what I've seen, believe me when I tell you that you're going to see one hell of a performance tonight and yes, I really am that good of an actress. Don told me so when we had lunch this afternoon. And, Katie, he's really great."

"Mel, you and Don? You just met him!"

"I know. I know. I'm flying back to L.A. Monday morning, and I have no idea where all of this might be going, but at my age I'm not about to turn down any opportunity for a little romantic adventure. Anyway, we'd better get back else the men are going to think we're snorting coke."

"In Abbeyville?" Katie laughed as the women left the seclusion of the powder room and returned to their seats.

The band began to play 70's classics and people filled the dance floor. Don was standing at the front door watching the scene, especially the couple who were dancing uncomfortably close. Uncomfortable for Don that is. The more he watched Melanie with Wyatt, the more he was beginning to feel that it had been a really bad idea to ask her to distract him while they completed the mission.

What she turned out to be, however, was his distraction from the mission, from his job, from just about everything he was supposed to be paying attention to. He was so deep in thought, he didn't notice Stuart trying to get his attention.

"Don. Don? DON."

"What? Oh sorry, Stu. I was listening to the music."

"Sure you were. Come back to earth, buddy. Did you hear that conversation between Wyatt, Eric and Charles?"

"Yes, it came through Melanie's communicator just fine. I think we should put a couple of agents on Eric and Charles. It sounded to me like Wyatt might have been threatening them and we can't take any chances until we have that weasel in custody."

"I didn't know we had given Wyatt the code name weasel."

"That's my own code name for Gaynes," Don smirked.

"I see. Well, it appears Melanie has things well in hand."

"So to speak."

"Yes, so to speak. I already spoke with Katie and James, and she's ready to leave whenever we need her. James is going to tell everyone that Katie isn't feeling well and is going home. He's going to stay here until the rest of the guests leave."

"I don't like getting so many civilians involved with us, Stu, but things seem to be going rather well as far as Wyatt not suspecting anything. Now that we have a way into his operation, and with Katie at UNCLE headquarters I'd say we're in a very good position to successfully complete the assignment."

"And say good-bye to small town Abbeyville. I can't wait to return to Paris. By the way, did you know the agency recently opened a headquarters in Los Angeles? You could apply for a transfer, if you had a good reason to relocate, that is."

"Yes, I know."

Don was thinking the very same thing as he watched his very good reason dancing a bit too closely with Wyatt Gaynes.

Chapter Sixteen

"Let's get the hell out of here."
Wyatt whispered into Melanie's ear as they were dancing.
She could smell the vodka on his breath and could tell by his slightly wavering stance that a great deal of the liquor served that night in the open bar had been consumed by Wyatt. She moved back a step and lightly brushed a bit of hair from his forehead
"Where did you have in mind?"
"I want to take you back to my place and give you the grand tour," Wyatt said. "I want you, and only you, to see what I've really accomplished over the past twenty years."
"Wyatt, you've already showed me your store. It's really nice and all, but I was thinking that maybe you'd like to come up to my hotel room where we could renew old acquaintances."
Melanie paused for a moment and waited for Wyatt's reaction. Much to her surprise, it seemed as if he wanted to impress her more with his business than with his sexual prowess.
"Oh, we'll have plenty of time for that, but first I want to show you what I've been hiding right under the noses of this stupid little town."
Wyatt was holding her a bit more forcefully than she liked. It was almost as if he was insisting she agree to go with him. The music stopped and when she tried to move away from him, he pulled her to him and gave her a long, passionate kiss, right in front of their entire former classmates, who further embarrassed her by giving them a congratulatory applause.
"Now, I really do want to leave," she said to Wyatt. "Let me say good-bye to Katie, get my purse and I'll meet you in the lobby."

"I'll be waiting by my car. If you're not there in exactly ten minutes, I'm coming back to get you."

Damn control freak, Melanie thought. As soon as Wyatt left the room, she quickly walked over to Katie's table. Seeing some of her classmates standing close-by, she had to be careful to tell Katie where she was going without alarming her.

"Wyatt had a few too many, and now he's insisting on taking me back to his place for something or other, so we're leaving. This was a great success, Katie. I really hate to have to leave early."

"Yes, so do I. Stuart is driving me to the bakery in about an hour." Katie lowered her voice. "He said the agents were going to be moving into Wyatt's, so you'd better be no where near that stationery store."

"Don't worry, I'll make sure Wyatt is safe and sound and back in my hotel room before the clock strikes midnight."

"When you'll turn him into a pumpkin?

"Or a werewolf!"

Melanie was on her way out the door when she saw Wyatt stagger back into the lobby.

"I said ten minutes."

"Damn, you are impatient, Wyatt. Give me your keys, you're in no condition to drive."

Wyatt started to protest, but seeing that Melanie wasn't going anywhere unless he agreed, he dropped the keys into her opened palm.

"That's better," She said. "Are you sure you want to go back to your place. It's getting late and I've already seen your store."

"Ah, you saw what I allow everyone else to see, but what I'm going to show you is nothing like you've ever seen before."

"Well if you insist. I'd much rather show you something you've never seen before."

Melanie ran her fingers down Wyatt's thigh.

"Oh, we'll have plenty of time for that after," Wyatt smiled.

"Then, we'd better be going."

Melanie was getting impatient. She knew she didn't have a lot of time before the agents would arrive, but she also knew she had to go along with Wyatt so he wouldn't become suspicious. She opened the car door for him, then walked around the back of the car to the driver's side, opened her purse and switched on the cigarette communicator, just in case.

Wyatt's erratic behavior was beginning to make her nervous. Her assignment to keep him occupied for the entire night wasn't going to be that difficult but now she had to get him into that occupied position back in her hotel room in less than an hour. Melanie turned the key in the ignition and drove the Mercedes toward town.

From the hotel lobby entranceway, Don watched the black sedan drive away. His first instinct was to jump in his car and follow, but once he noticed that Melanie had switched on the communicator, he knew that she was in control and if there was any trouble, he would be alerted.

There were other agents in close proximity to Wyatt's store, waiting for the signal to enter and start their mission and Don needed to drive Katie back to UNCLE headquarters to get her ready to receive the information once the agents were in position and able to transmit.

It was times like these when his job was the most difficult, he thought. Although all the plans were in place, until the moment when the operation began, there was no way of knowing if they would succeed, and the waiting was the hardest. He would go over every detail again and again in his mind, and play out all possible scenarios, but in some cases, the unexpected happened and they would lose good agents. However, in all his years with UNCLE, Don had never lost a civilian, nor fallen in love with one.

He located Stuart and they quietly met Katie, who was doing a fantastic job of faking stomach cramps. Don watched as James escorted her from the hotel. Once they were outside, Katie miraculously recovered.

"Mel isn't the only one who can act," she said. "She told me that her and Wyatt were going back to his store, but she said she would make sure to have him out of there by midnight."

"I'm not going to ask how she is going to do that," said James.

With a little bit of drugged champagne, I hope. Don thought.

"Let's get going," Don said. "We have a long night ahead of us. Thanks, James. Don't worry, we'll take good care of her."

"You'd better, or I'll have every state and federal agency on your ass."

As the men drove off, James headed back to the party. Several people came up to him and asked how Katie was feeling. He told them that she probably was just a bit stressed because of all the work she did for the reunion. That comment produced many words of deserved praise for his wife. He only wished that she had been there to hear it for herself.

James knew he was a very lucky man, but he didn't realize how much he depended on Katie until he was faced with the possibility of losing her forever. It shouldn't have taken chest pains, or hearing about her involvement with a secret organization, to make him appreciate her, but once they got through the next few days, he vowed he would never again take her for granted.

Across the room, Eric and Charles were trying to have a private conversation. Unfortunately the band picked that exact moment to crank up the volume to an uncomfortable level, so they were forced to move out to the patio so they could hear each other talk.

"Eric, I'm very concerned about the way Wyatt's been acting this week. I've never seen him so... I can't even put a word on it."

"Megalomaniac?"

"Yeah, Mega - whatever. You're the damn writer."

"Don't remind me," Eric took a huge gulp of scotch. "I tried to tell him that too much press coverage was going to raise a lot of questions, but he was insistent. I would have thought getting that Senate bill out of the way would have made him relax, especially after I wrote that bogus article repudiating all the scientific facts."

"You should have just returned the Pulitzer when you found out about what Wyatt was up to. That prize came with some very heavy strings, and now we're both stuck."

"I thought your kids received full scholarships after Wyatt paid their first year tuition. That should have gotten you off the hook, Chuck."

"Except for the one little fact that Wyatt also bribed the scholarship committees and falsified the transcripts."

"You're kidding me. Shit, man. I think I need a refill. Be right back."

"Here, I need one, too," Charles handed his empty glass to Eric who took the empties to the bar. A moment later he returned.

"We need to stop this guy before he gets caught and pulls us down with him," Eric said.

"I agree," Charles replied. "This morning, Wyatt held a meeting and told everyone that the international representatives were arriving tomorrow and that everything was going according to his schedule, whatever the hell that means. I wrote all the programs, so my part of this is finished. Once those presses start rolling, we're both screwed."

"You know how to get into his communication base, right?" Eric asked.

"Of course, I've been working in that rat trap for the past eighteen months." Chuck spat out his words.

"No one is going to be there on a Sunday morning, right?"

Eric was beginning to form a plan.

"As far as I know, no one is scheduled at all tomorrow. I think Wyatt wanted to make it look like he'd done this entirely on his own."

Chuck downed his drink in one swallow.

"The reunion brunch is at eleven tomorrow. I know Wyatt will be there because he's hosting the event. Katie told us, that was Wyatt's big contribution to the reunion committee. He even added his name to the invitation, even though his only effort was writing the check, he'll definitely be here and not at his base of operations," Eric said.

"And we'll be at the base before the brunch. I know enough about that place to throw a nice little virus into the mix. We'll arrive a bit late to the brunch and by that time Wyatt won't know what hit him."

Charles raised his glass. "Here's to our freedom, the end of THRUSH and the end of Wyatt Gaynes."

Eric clicked his glass to Charles'.

"I'll drink to that, and make it a double."

The streets of Abbeyville were shut tight after ten nearly every night and this Saturday was no exception. Melanie had no problem finding a place to park Wyatt's car since it was the only vehicle on the street. It worried her for a few seconds that if anything were to happen to her, there wouldn't be any witnesses. Then she remembered the communicator in her purse and that in less than an hour, Wyatt's place would be crawling with UNCLE agents. She was also happy to see that the fresh air had seemed to have sober Wyatt as he exited his side of the car and opened her door.

"Aren't you the gentleman?"

She put on a fake smile. It was going to be a very long night if she had to keep up the pretense.

"You deserve nothing less, m'lady. I'm happy you agreed to come with me. When we were here earlier, there were too many strangers around and even my employees don't know about this place. Follow me."

Melanie pretended she didn't know anything about the alley entrance, and although she knew the way, it was extremely difficult to walk on gravel in three-inch heels.

"You're going to really love this."

Wyatt pressed the code which opened the door. "The combination isn't my birthday, or any other common number. Do you know what I keyed the code to?"

Melanie moved her purse a bit closer so Don would be able to hear everything. "I have no idea, Wyatt."

"It's your birthday, Mel. 01201954."

Melanie was actually surprised, more like shocked. "Wyatt, how on earth did you remember that, and why on earth would you remember that?"

"You'd be surprised at what I remember, Mel. C'mon, this is really going to impress you."

"Uh, do I need to take off my shoes, Wyatt?"

He gave her a warm laugh, "No, not down here. C'mon"

Melanie followed Wyatt into the electronics room where she had seen him with Chuck and the others earlier. The pins on the world map were lit on several counties, andt Melanie was relieved to see that the native language of the majority of them were variations of the English language. The rest of the accents she could easily fake.

Wyatt gave her the grand tour of the electronics operation, but he didn't stop there. He led her into an elevator and pressed the 5L button. The lower the car descended, the more anxious she became. When the elevator doors finally opened, Melanie was stunned to see an underground canal with six yellow mini subs moored on the edge.

"Wyatt, this is incredible!"

"My very own aqueduct. I told you you'd be impressed."

"You were right."

And so was Don, she thought.

"How long has this been here?" she asked.

Melanie needed more information and Wyatt was more than happy to provide it.

"For years. It was built way back when the papermill was in Abbeyville, the company would have the lumber delivered by water. It was a lot less expensive than by truck, but once Jack took over, he shut down the entire water route. I re-opened it for my operation and had the subs painted yellow. You know I've always been a Beatles fan."

"Yes, I remember, but whatever would you need to transport through an aqueduct?"

Melanie hoped all her questions wouldn't raise Wyatt's suspicions. She was relying on his bravado to get him to reveal more information. He didn't disappoint her.

"I have several business associates who don't feel comfortable going through the front door, or can't because they have less than impeccable rap sheets. I also transport certain products that haven't exactly been cleared through U.S. or Canadian customs that I need for, well, let's just say that some of the special orders need a higher quality of paper from the mill that isn't exactly legal to import or export."

Melanie was definitely hoping that Don was getting all this through her communicator, but as she looked around, she noticed the concrete walls appeared to be extremely thick. She was beginning to feel a bit claustrophobic. She started walking towards what she thought was the exit door when Wyatt abruptly grabbed her arm.

"NO!" Wyatt shouted, startling her.

Seeing her reaction, Wyatt immediately lowered his voice and tried to offer an explanation.

"Sorry, Mel. I didn't mean to scare you, but you can't go that way. That's where all the heavy printing equipment is and I wouldn't want you to get hurt."

Melanie's trained ear picked up a slight threat in Wyatt's voice, then he changed it as soon as she started walking back toward him.

"Isn't this the greatest thing you've ever seen?"

Wyatt suddenly sounded like a little kid who had just received an "A" and was looking for mommy's approval. Not one to disappoint, Melanie was more than happy to give Wyatt the praise he seemed so desperate to hear.

"Wyatt, I am truly amazed. You have created something here that you should be very proud of, but if you don't mind, it's a bit damp down here and I don't want to catch cold. How about driving me back to the hotel where I can show you exactly how impressed I am?"

Melanie started walking toward the elevator door, when Wyatt took her arm and re-directed her to one on the opposite side of the room.

"This elevator goes directly to my apartment, Mel. We don't need to drive all the way to your hotel."

Melanie had to think fast. She knew that the UNCLE agents would be there in less than fifteen minutes and going up to Wyatt's apartment was not an option.

"That would be nice, Wyatt, but I'd really like to get out of this dress and into something, shall I use the cliché, more comfortable. Like the huge shower in my hotel room. The one with massaging jets that's big enough for two?"

C'mon Wyatt, Melanie thought. Take the bait. She followed her invitation with a deep kiss, pressing herself tightly to his body, her left hand moved slowly to just below his belt.

"We can order a bottle of champagne from room service and celebrate the renewed passion of old friends."

"Sounds delicious Mel, but we don't have to order overpriced hotel champagne. I have a complete wine cellar over there and always keep several bottles of champagne chilled just in case I have some reason to celebrate. I can't think of anything I'd rather celebrate than you and I renewing our passion as you said. Be back in a sec."

With Wyatt out of sight, Melanie checked the cigarette case, making sure the LED was still lit indicating that the transmission did, indeed penetrate the concrete. She let out the breath she had been holding since she entered the elevator.

Wyatt returned with two bottles of Dom Perigon. Melanie took them from him in exchange for his car keys.

"Let's make some new memories that will last until the next reunion, or longer," she said.

They rode the elevator to the top floor. Melanie was desperately trying not to check her watch, but once they reached the street, she was relieved to see that they had only spend forty-five minutes inside, leaving plenty of time for a now sober Wyatt to drive them back to her hotel before the agents arrived

As soon as they closed the car door, Wyatt hit the gas and raced toward the hotel. For a brief moment Melanie was reminded of the last time she was sitting in the passenger side of Wyatt's car as they sped to a sleazy motel on Route Ten. The memory of that night was something that she had haunted her for many years. Now, Don had given her a golden opportunity to exorcize all of those ghosts once and for all and she wasn't going to waste it.

With her left hand, Melanie reached over and caressed Wyatt's thigh. With her right, she caressed her purse which contained the capsule of knock-out drug.

In that moment, Melanie Tyler was no longer reliving the memories of a being screwed by the high school quarterback. She was an agent of UNCLE, on a mission to stop Wyatt Gaynes from screwing the entire world.

Chapter Seventeen

Melanie wasn't worried that Wyatt wouldn't accept her invitation to return to her hotel room as much as she was concerned that she might not be able to fake her desire to spend the entire night with him. Good actors needed to believe the role and the character they were portraying in order to convince their audience. Bad actors never could pull it off. In order for Melanie to succeed in her deception, she knew a small part of her needed to believe it too.

She decided to relax and get into the role for an audience of one. Wyatt was driving the car with his left hand on the wheel and his right dangerously close to her upper thigh. She gently removed it and placed it back on the wheel, then put her hand on the exact same position on his thigh.

"This is only a prelude to the symphony I have in store for us later, Wyatt. For now I think you should keep both hands on the wheel, and your eyes on the road. I wouldn't want to have to explain to the cops what we were going when you hit a fire hydrant."

"This town is so boring, Mel, that would probably be the most thrill the cop, or anyone else, has had in decades."

"Does that include you?" she asked.

"Me? You're kidding right? I head to the twin cities almost every weekend. There's been a few women who wanted to be Mrs. Gaynes, but they couldn't put up..."

"With your ego?" Melanie joked.

"I was going to say my work schedule. Sometimes I burn the midnight oil until the sun comes up. Only take a break to for a quick shower and an even quicker nap, then head back to the office. Doesn't leave much time for romance."

"Well, tonight you're not going to be working and we'll have plenty of time for, well, let's just say we'll have plenty of time," she purred.

Wyatt parked the car and this time Melanie opened her own door. She grabbed her purse and Wyatt carried the bottles of champagne and flutes into the lobby, which was, thankfully empty.

As soon as the elevator doors closed, Wyatt's lips were on Melanie's and his hands were firmly planted on her ass. Fortunately, she was able to retrieve the room key from her purse without Wyatt seeing the other items that were hidden inside. After they entered the room, she barely had the door closed when Wyatt reached down and pulled her very expensive designer dress over her head, then left it in a crumpled pile on the floor. He tried to kiss her, but she pulled back.

"Damn, you are impatient, aren't you?" Melanie picked up the dress and laid it over a nearby chair. "I'd like some champagne first, Wyatt. I'll open the bottle and you go wait for me in the bedroom."

"I like your waiting on me, Mel, but don't keep me waiting too long," Wyatt said as he handed her the bottle and the glasses. "I've been looking forward to this since I first saw you at the cocktail party."

"I've been looking forward to this for twenty years," she whispered the half truth.

In fact, she had been waiting for this moment for decades, but it certainly wasn't the same moment that Wyatt was referring.

"Go get undressed. I'll join you in a sec."

Once Wyatt was safely out of sight, Melanie took the capsule from her purse and dropped it into one of the flutes, then filled both with champagne. She glanced at the clock and was surprised to see it was only a few minutes past midnight.

Don had told her the agents needed at least four hours to complete their mission, but it had been a little less that two since she and Wyatt had left the party and there was still a good five hours left to detain him. She hoped Don was right about the drug. The thought of her having to go through with a real seduction wasn't something Melanie was that eager to do.

She brought the glasses into the bedroom where she found Wyatt relaxing on the bed wearing only his briefs. She sat next to him, clinked her glass on his and took a long sip of her champagne.

"Would you like to join me in the hot shower? Those wall jets are wonderful."

Melanie hoped the drug would take effect before Wyatt had an opportunity to take her up on her offer. But she had a more urgent problem if Don had been wrong about the effectiveness of the drug.

"As much as I would like to spend the rest of the evening taking you to ecstasy in the shower, and in the living room and all over this suite, I have to get back to the office by seven tomorrow morning. I wasn't kidding when I said I could never have a decent relationship because I'm a workaholic. I hate to rush this excellent champagne, but, bottoms up."

Wyatt emptied the glass in one large gulp, then he moved a few inches on the bed and patted the mattress as an invitation for Melanie to lie down next to him. She very slowly removed her bra and panties, all the while watching Wyatt watch her. She crawled into the bed, elongating her body so that every inch of her bare skin was touching his. He began kissing her and she tentatively responded until she felt his body go limp as the drug finally took effect.

Melanie looked at the sleeping face of the man lying beside here and wondered what had happened to the young innocent boy she thought she once loved. What terrible influence had driven him to want money and power so much that he was willing to do anything to get it.

Maybe Wyatt's life would have turned out differently if she hadn't waited for him to call her and had, instead, made that call herself. Maybe she wouldn't have left for California, maybe he would have come with her, or maybe they would have simply dated for a few months then gone their separate ways.

Oh well, it was much too late for the shoulda, coulda, woulda, didn't regrets, she thought as she

pulled the blanket over Wyatt's now passed-out body. She grabbed her robe from the closet, set the alarm for six-thirty and went to sleep on the outer-room couch.

On the other side of town, Don was doing his best not to think about Melanie and Wyatt and what she might be doing to keep him occupied. Instead, he tried to concentrate on getting Katie connected to the phone lines and computer transmissions that were beginning to come through.

"It looks like it's working, Katie." he said watching the computer screens.

"Did you have any doubt?" Katie replied. "No matter how complicated people think computer language is, it's never really been that far from the basic one and zero that started it all. You can tell your agents that I've succeeded in hacking into Wyatt's mainframe and you now have complete access to his entire system."

"Katie, you really missed your calling. Our agents have been trying to crack this for months," Stuart said.

"You have to remember it was Chuck who programmed all of this, and he's no genius. I think the only reason Wyatt got him to do it, was that he didn't have to pay him the hourly rate, and you get what you pay for. Wait till I send you guys my bill."

Katie watched as the last files finished downloading. She felt proud of herself that she had been able to break Chuck's codes so easily, and equally glad to know that her

UNCLE adventure was coming to an end. While it had been an interesting experience, all she ever really wanted out of life was to have a nice normal family, a home, and the love of a great man.

The life of a spy wasn't something she would ever had chosen for herself. Katie was glad she was able to help the agents, but she was anxious to get back to her real life.

"Whatever Melanie did to keep Wyatt distracted, we owe her," Stuart said. "I told her to meet us here at seven so she can get connected to the phone system."

Yeah, whatever she did. Don thought. "Well, it's only six-thirty, and there's no sign of Wyatt. So far things are going exactly as planned. Katie, can you stay awake long enough to wait until Melanie gets here?"

"If you have coffee, I'd love a cup. And maybe run up to the bakery and pick up some fresh donuts. I can be bribed, don't cha know. But I have to tell you guys, I'm looking forward to a very long hot bath when we're done."

"You got it, Katie. I'll be right back," Stuart said.

Several minutes later he returned with the coffee and donuts. They watched the video screen and saw the UNCLE operatives leave Wyatt's location. Now, all they had to do was wait for Melanie to join them and for Wyatt to walk into their trap.

After more than five years of watching and waiting, Operation Wyatt Gaynes was about to finally come to an end. For Don, it couldn't have come any sooner. Once Wyatt was in custody, and THRUSH was once again destroyed, he was thinking it might be time to take a nice desk job. Maybe in a much warmer climate.

Like Southern California.

Chapter Eighteen

Although she hadn't been able to sleep for more than a few hours, Melanie was wide awake ten minutes before the alarm went off. Sneaking into the bedroom, she was relieved to see that Wyatt was still asleep. She dropped the robe on the floor and crawled into the bed. Lying her full naked body against his, she ran her fingers lightly over his chest, and whispered,

"Wake up, sleepy-head."

Wyatt opened his eyes and looked around the room trying to remember exactly where he was. Seeing Melanie lying next to him, he turned to kiss her, but she backed away.

"Let's not start something we can't finish, Wyatt. You said you had an important meeting, at seven remember?"

"Damn, girl. I don't remember anything. That must have been some champagne. What time is it?"

"Six-thirty. What do you mean you don't remember anything? Wyatt, you were fantastic!" Melanie lied.

"I was?" Wyatt was struggling to remember the events that hadn't happened. "Of course I was." he said. "I was worth the wait, wasn't I, Melanie?"

"Definitely Wyatt. I've been waiting twenty years to do exactly what we did last night." She suppressed a laugh. "I'm so sore, I can hardly move."

Wyatt's Cheshire Cat grin was more than Melanie could stomach but she had to continue playing the part of a very satisfied lover if Wyatt was going to believe her story.

"Why don't you take a shower and I'll order breakfast," In a faked-pleading voice which she knew Wyatt loved, she added, "I'm sure you can reschedule your meeting for me, can't you, Wyatt? Please?"

She already knew the answer.

"Sorry, Mel. As much as I'd like to stay," he glanced at the bulge forming under the sheets, "As much as I'd really really like to stay, I'm afraid that I'll have to take a rain check. I'll see you later at the farewell brunch."

Not if you're in jail, you won't.

Wyatt gave her a light kiss on her forehead then, without saying another word, quickly dressed, then rushed out of the hotel room with a small wave and a non-committal "See ya later."

As soon as door closed, Melanie picked up her cell and pressed the UNCLE number she'd entered into the phone's memory earlier. Don answered on the first ring.

"Wyatt just left," she said. "I'm going to wait another five minutes, then I'll join you."

Don was secretly relieved to hear Melanie's voice on the other end.

"We're all waiting for you, Mel," Don said. "I take it everything went according to plan?"

He held his breath waiting for her reply.

"Yes, Don. Everything went exactly as you planned. Wyatt and I slept together."

There was a very long pause. Then, with a bit of laugher in her voice, she answered his unasked question.

"I said we slept, Don. The drug worked perfectly. When Wyatt woke up this morning, I told him what a fantastic lover he was and of course he believed every word. He even said he was sorry he couldn't remember and that he must have had more to drink then he thought. I just told him that I will always remember our very special night together, which is very true. I'll always remember how that guy can shore! Damn, I really am that good of an actress."

"Of that I had no doubt, Melanie," Don said. "How soon can you get here?"

"Soon as I'm dressed. I should be there in about ten minutes."

"GREAT!"

He replied with a bit too much enthusiasm in his voice. Both Stuart and Katie were startled by his response. Don tried, without much success to cover up his slip.

"That was Melanie."

He told Stuart after the call ended.

"She said Wyatt just left and she'll be here in a few minutes. I just said that was great news."

"Right." Neither Stuart nor Katie believed him for one second.

It was nearly seven by the time Melanie joined them in the UNCLE control room. She'd changed into jeans and a hooded sweatshirt and looked surprisingly well rested even though she hadn't gotten much sleep.

"Wyatt should be at his place any minute."

Melanie said, trying not to look at Don who was also trying not to look at her. "I took a short cut through the side streets so he wouldn't see me. It was also a lot quicker. I hope you guys were able to get everything set-up."

Just as she finished the sentence, the video cameras that the agents had positioned in the alley began broadcasting onto the split screen in front of them. The image on one showed Wyatt entering the entrance to his store. The second screen followed him into his back office where they watched him sit down and pick up the phone. As soon as Wyatt dialed the first number, the light on the console in front of Melanie lit bright red, and the telephone number came on the screen, identifying the location of the call.

"Ok, Mel. You're on. This one is easy. The country code is Ireland."

Melanie waited until the third ring before she picked up the call. In perfect Irish brogue, she answered all of Wyatt's questions and assured him that Mr. Shaunessy, whoever he was, was on his way to the United States and would arrive at the scheduled time of seven p.m.

"Now we know the location of his operation in Ireland," Don said. "And the exact time when the meeting is," Stu added. "You're doing great, Mel. You sounded like a native."

"That's why they pay me the big bucks," she replied. "Is there any more coffee? I'm not nearly as awake as I look."

Stuart handed her a cup, but before she had a chance to take a sip, the light went on again. This time the location was France. Fortunately, Melanie was fluent in Spanish, Italian and French due to the many voice classes she had to take to perfect her various voice-over accents. The screen also showed that the time in France was four-thirty in the afternoon, so Melanie answered with a bon jour before switching to English with a heavy French accent.

Melanie expertly imitated the accents of the rest of the thirteen countries that composed the European Union. Some of her voices were high and feminine, others were more deep and could have been either male or female. Katie, Don and Stu could see that all the voices were coming from Melanie's lips, but if they hadn't been in the same room, they would have thought that there were fourteen different people answering the phone.

Two hours later, the line went dark.

"I think Wyatt's finished making his calls," Melanie said, "Dare I say, mission accomplished?"

"Well, I wouldn't want to celebrate prematurely," Stuart said.

"Or, for that matter, do anything else prematurely," Don joked, tossing a look toward Mel who smiled in response.

"Ok, you two, get a room already," Katie said. "If we're done here, I need a hot bath and a very long overdue nap."

"We'll have our agents positioned at Wyatt's at seven-fifteen tonight, right after all his operatives arrive. They've all gone home for the day and we're in the process of closing down THRUSH once and for all, thanks to the two of you."

Melanie opened her purse, retrieved the gun, cigarette case, communicator pen and ID badge and handed them to Don. "I guess I won't be needing these anymore."

"I'm glad you didn't have to use this," Don picked up the revolver.

Really glad, he thought. He put the gun and badge into a drawer, but left the cigarette case and pen in Melanie's hand.

"These will be deactivated once you leave this room," Don said. "But I thought you should have something to remember us by."

Melanie put the items into the front pocket of her sweatshirt.

"Thanks, Don, but I'll probably quit again when I get home," She said. "The entire state has outlawed smoking, but I can always use another pen to sign autographs," she smiled.

"Oooh, big star!" Katie joked, "I just need a pen to sign all of those checks I need to pay for the reunion, thanks."

"Well, since it appears we're done," Melanie said. "I think I'll head back to the hotel and take a nap before the farewell brunch. I'd still like to get in some actual reunion time if only to say good-bye to a few friends before they leave."

"I think I'm going to skip the brunch," Katie yawned. "I need a long nap and some quality alone time with my husband."

"So, I guess I'll say good-bye to you now, Katie."Rehearsals have already started for the fall season and my flight leaves first thing tomorrow morning."

Melanie gave her friend a long good-bye hug. Over her shoulder, she looked at Don to see if there was any indication that he was going to wish her a good trip, or, better still, ask her to stay a bit longer, but he was putting away the files and didn't even notice. Instead, Stuart began walking toward the exit.

"Thank you ladies, for all your help. Don and I have a few loose ends to tie up and I think we both need to take a shower."

Don put the last of the papers into the filing cabinet and walked over to join Stuart as he started escorting the women to the elevator.

"And I know I need to shave," Don rubbed the stubble on his chin. He put the last paper into the filing cabinet, pushed the drawer closed and reached Melanie's side in two steps. When she turned to face him, his eyes connected with hers and with one sentence, Melanie's hopes were about to come true.

"I'll stop by the hotel tonight, Mel. I really would like to see you before you leave."

Finally

"After you shave," she smiled.

Melanie followed her two former classmates into the elevator. Stuart thanked the women once again for their help, told them he would see them again at their next reunion in ten years, got into his car and waved to both the women as he drove away.

"I'm almost sorry that our little adventure is over," Melanie said to Katie.

"Are you sorry the adventure is over, or that your little flirting game with Don is over?"

"I wouldn't exactly say it was over," Melanie said. "He did say he'd come to the hotel later to say good-bye."

"Or convince you not to leave?" Katie smiled. "Can I ride with you back to the hotel? I drove here with Stuart. My truck is still in the hotel parking lot."

"Of course. Hey, you want to drive by Wyatt's store one last time?" Melanie said.

"Are you crazy? I would think you had enough of that creep."

"I'm just curious if anything changed since we sabotaged his operation."

"You really are enjoying playing spy, aren't you?" Katie said. "Hollywood action flicks not exciting enough?

"My agent never sent me on any spy audition roles, so I guess this is as close as I'll ever get to the part. Maybe I'll be able to use this experience as research in case I'm ever up for an action role. Ya never know!"

"Ok, just to satisfy your curiosity. Then straight to the hotel so I can get home."

Melanie began driving toward Wyatt's store. They were about a half block away when Melanie pulled over and stopped the car.

"Katie! Isn't that Charles and Eric? They're heading toward the alley."

"If Charles gets into the computer server, he'll notice that we've downloaded all the files," Katie said. "he'll tell Wyatt, and he'll cancel the meeting!"

"And everything we've done will be for nothing!"

The women were beginning to panic.

"Katie, we have to tell Don." Melanie took the communicator pen from her pocket, but when she pulled out the antenna, the light didn't turn on. She tried the cigarette case, but it also failed to activate.

"Mel, Don said the communicators were turned off. I left my cell in the truck that's parked at the hotel."

"Damn. I left mine in the hotel," Melanie said. "We'll think of something later, but right now we have to try and stop Chuck and Eric. C'mon."

Before Katie could protest, Melanie jumped from the car and started running across the street. Katie followed her into the alley and through the back door that led to Wyatt's computer room. Once they were inside, the women moved slowly, keeping a safe distance from the two men who were directly in front of them. Melanie noticed that the world map on the wall which had been lit the last time she had seen it, was now completely dark. Charles was running around checking all the wire connections. Melanie and Katie knew it would only be a matter of time before he discovered their sabotage. They had to act fast, even if it meant exposing themselves.

Stepping out from behind the wall, Melanie said, "What do you guys think you're doing?"

Eric nearly jumped from his seat when he saw the women.

"What are we doing?" Charles stammered. "I work here. What are you two doing? How did you get in?"

Charles was about to check the computer hook-ups when Katie distracted him.

"We followed you, sneaking around like thieves. You looked like you were trying to break in." Katie noticed there were several wires on the floor by her feet, and she carefully nudged them with her toe and pushed them under the console.

"Wyatt asked me to check some...uh...systems he was worried about, but so far we can't seem to find anything out of the ordinary," Charles lied. "Except the lights on the map aren't working, other than the one showing the location of Abbeyville."

"And what is Eric doing here?" Katie needed to keep both of them from seeing a few loose cables that the UNCLE hadn't secured.

"I wanted to see Wyatt's operation, so I can write a business profile on him, that's all." Eric lied.

"I suggest we all get out of here before Wyatt discovers us snooping around this place."

Before the men had a chance to respond, Melanie heard an all-too familiar voice directly behind her.

"Wyatt has already discover you snooping around this place. Now he just wants to know exactly why you're snooping around my place."

Melanie turned around to see Wyatt, still dressed in his tux. The expression on his face was nothing like she had seen only a few hours earlier. He was aiming something at them that she was certain wasn't an indicator that he was at all happy to see her.

In her sweetest, most seductive voice, Melanie said, "Wyatt, put that gun away. There's a perfectly good explanation..."

"I can see that from where I'm standing. It looks like the four of you are here to interfere with my master plan."

He directed his words to the men.

"You two were such gullible fools, so happy to take my money and use my family's influence when you needed it and this is how you repay me? By going behind my back and trying to sabotage my operation, Chuckie?"

"Not me, Wyatt. I've been working for you for years. Why would you think that I'd do anything like that?"

Charles wasn't at all convincing.

"I really don't care why you four are here, but I can't have any witnesses. Sorry, Mel. After last night, this isn't what I had in mind for a second date. Now, all four of you, start walking through that door and down the stairs."

"Second date?" Katie whispered to Melanie. "What exactly did you do with Wyatt last night? I thought you said nothing happened."

"Shhh, Wyatt doesn't know that," Melanie whispered back.

Halfway down the stairs, Eric suddenly turned and confronted Wyatt. "I'm not going anywhere. You're not man enough to shoot us, Mr. Silver."

Wyatt pointed the gun toward Eric and pulled the trigger. The bullet flew just past his left ear and hit the ceiling.

"Next time you call me Mr. Silver, I won't miss. Now keep moving!"

Melanie notices that Wyatt's voice lacked any emotion and his eyes were ice cold. When they reached the bottom of the stairs, Wyatt pressed a concrete block which opened a door leading into a dark, clammy room. He switched on the two bare bulbs in the ceiling.

As soon as the four were inside, he said, "Give me your cell phones. These walls are ten feet thick, but I'm not taking any chances."

Charles and Eric took their phones from their pants pocket and handed them to Wyatt.

"I suppose you don't care if I leave my shoes on in here, do you, you shit."

"You're right, Melanie. About the shoes I mean, not about my being a shit."

"My mistake. Calling you a shit is an insult to shits everywhere."

"Cute. Now, hand over your cell phone before I totally forget about what a great time we had last night."

"Sorry, Wyatt, but I left my cell phone in the hotel room. See? No purse, and no pants pockets."

Melanie turned around so Wyatt wouldn't check her sweatshirt pocket. She was silently kicking herself for returning the gun Don had given her.

Wyatt took their phones.

"There isn't any way to escape, so don't bother trying. It's soundproof, too, so I suggest you don't waste whatever air you have left in here crying for help. I just need you out of the way for awhile, so sit tight, I'll be back in a few hours."

Wyatt turned to leave, but just before he closed the concrete door he turned around, stared directly into the faces of his prisoners and, in a chilling tone added, "or maybe I won't."

There was a moment of terrifying silence, then Charles let out an ear shattering scream.

"I DON'T WANT TO DIE!"

Chapter Nineteen
Present Day

Chuck's desperate cries pierced through Melanie's retrospective, bringing her back to their present predicament.

"Once again, Chuck, we're not going to die. Would you please just shut up already?"

Katie was continuing to feel for any cracks in the concrete.

"Dammit. If only that bastard hadn't taken our cell phones," he yelled.

"I doubt we'd be able to get any service from within these walls, anyway," Eric added. "We're so screwed. I never should have trusted Wyatt."

"Eric, let's face it, Wyatt played us all from the start and we fell for it. We'll deal with him after we get out of here."

"IF we get out of here," Charles cried.

"SHUT UP, CHUCK!" Melanie and Katie yelled in unison.

"Now I know why you followed us into Wyatt's offices. You two were playing spies, like when we were kids. You always did have quite an overly active imagination back then. No wonder you wanted to be an actress, Mel" Eric shot back.

"You tell her, Eric," Charles joined in the verbal attack. "See where all your stupid playing around got us. We're locked in a basement by an egomaniac with a loaded gun pointed at our heads. Let's see if your spy movies can get us out of this one, Agents Tyler and Conner."

"That's agent O'Brien, Chuckie." Katie said. "I have an idea. Melanie, you still have that cigarette case, right?"

"Yes, Wyatt didn't think to check my front pocket."

"Good, give me one."

"Katie, you don't smoke. I know you're upset, but now is not a good time to start."

"I'm not going to actually smoke it, just light it."

"You won't inhale, right." Eric snapped.

Ignoring his comment, Melanie took the cigarette case from her sweatshirt pocket and handed it to Katie. She opened the case, took out a cigarette, and pulled apart the cover, revealing the knife. Eric and Charles stared at her with a mixture of disbelief and amusement.

"That's real cute, Mel," Eric snapped, "What else do you have hidden under your sweatshirt?"

"A hell of a lot more then you have inside your pants, Eric," Melanie replied.

"That's for sure."

Katie wasn't accustomed to sexual innuendos, and she was grateful that the darkness in the room concealed her embarrassment.

"Ignore them, Katie. With any luck we'll be out of here in a few minutes. I don't know what I hate Wyatt for more, putting us into this room, or putting us into this room with those two."

"The feeling is still mutual on that point," Charles said. "What exactly do you think you're doing, Katie?"

"Just be quite and watch."

Katie lit the cigarette with the lighter on the case and lowered herself to the floor. She exhaled the smoke on the cracks between the floor and the walls, until she found the one place where the smoke went through to the outside.

"Here, I found the opening. Mel, take the blade and follow the smoke up the crack, hopefully it will release the latch."

"Like using a credit card to break open a door." Eric said.

"I'm sure you would know all about that, Eric." Katie snapped.

As Katie continued to exhale, Melanie traced the line of smoke with the blade until she heard the click of an opening latch. She gave the case one hard pull and the door opened, letting in welcoming light of freedom.

"Let's get out of here!"

Eric yelled. He and Charles nearly knocked over the women as they scrambled toward the stairs.

"Sheesh, not even a thank you." Katie said, handing the cigarette case back to Melanie. "Don't let anyone ever tell you that smoking will kill you. Sometimes, it will actually save your life."

The women started up the stairs when they were suddenly met by a familiar and very worried face.

"Stuart! You found us!" Katie cried.

"How did you know where we were?" asked Melanie.

"We called James to see if you had gotten home Katie and when he said you hadn't yet arrived, we sent a team over to the hotel and they discovered your truck was still parked there. Melanie's car has a tracking system, so it wasn't difficult to find where you parked. Once we saw the car, we traced the transmitter in the cigarette case and here we are. We were expecting to rescue you, but apparently you didn't need us."

"Like hell we didn't!" Melanie said. "Katie was brilliant, but if we had to be trapped in that room with those two jerks for one minute longer, you would have had to rescue them from us!"

Stuart laughed.

"Let's get you all out of here. We'll deal with those guys later. They won't get very far, we have about two dozen agents in the vicinity."

The women followed Stuart up the stairs and into the light, pausing for a second to take a few deep, clean breaths. After being cooped-up with the men, and no ventilation, the aroma in the room was none too pleasant

"Damn, do I ever need to take a hot shower," Melanie let out a hug yawn. "And brush my teeth!"

"I agree," replied Kate. "I've been up for almost twenty-four hours straight and I'm exhausted."

"What were you girls thinking going back into Wyatt's place without any back-up?" Stuart said.

"I guess we weren't thinking. Sorry Stu. Maybe we should leave the spy game to the professionals. Speaking of professionals, where is Don?"

Melanie hoped she didn't sound too disappointed.

"He was right behind me when we went in to get you. I just received a message from him that he picked up Eric and Charles as they were leaving."

"You mean as they were running away liked scared rabbits," Melanie said.

"Don took them back to headquarters for interrogation, I mean questioning. I'm sure they have a ton of information on Wyatt that will help us convict him, once he's in custody that is."

"You mean to tell me you haven't arrested him yet?" Katie was stunned.

"Not yet, but soon. We're waiting for the rest of his organization to arrive. As we found out with your help, Melanie, the meeting isn't until seven tonight, and we want to get all of them, not just their leader." Don said.

"In spite of all the unexpected activities, it's been a very nice reunion, Katie."

"Thanks, Stu. Let's not do this again in ten years. I still need that ride back to my car, Melanie?"

"Sure, and this time we won't take any detours."

Stuart headed back to UNCLE headquarters, Katie and Melanie drove off in the opposite direction.

"This certainly has been some kind of adventure," Melanie said. "I still can't believe what just happened. I'm still not convinced that this whole scenario wasn't some kind of practical joke."

"Believe me, Mel," Katie said. "This wasn't a joke. What James told me about Wyatt, well, let's just say if we hadn't opened that concrete door when we did I wasn't all that certain we'd get out of there alive."

"Still Katie, I feel that we missed something. Don't you think it was all somehow too easy. I mean, I'm a voice over actress, you're a PTA stay-at-home mom and suddenly we're super spies who brought down an international criminal and his entire organization?"

"You're just over tired, Mel, and maybe a bit paranoid. I think you're still looking at all of this like it's some Hollywood movie. Real life, especially real life in Abbeyville, is still pretty boring."

"That's what Wyatt said, too."

Melanie stopped her car by Katie's truck. Just before leaving Katie said, "I'm just thankful it's over. Thanks for the ride, Mel. I've had enough reunion for at least ten more years. I'm going home, getting into a hot tub and going to soak the memory of all this off my body. With any luck it will go down the drain along with the dirty water."

"Maybe you're right," Melanie replied. "I should probably finish packing. This was definitely not the relaxing weekend I had planned."

"Have a safe flight," Katie said. "I'll call you in a few days to find out how your date with Don went."

"If there is a date," Melanie said. "Don still hasn't called to confirm or to see how I am after we escaped from Wyatt's. I'm beginning to think he was only pretending to be interested in me so that I'd finish the assignment."

"Mel, if you can't trust a spy, who can you trust?"

"I guess you have a point, Katie. Get home and get some rest."

After Katie drove off, Mel started walking toward the hotel. She still couldn't ignore the nagging ache in her gut that was telling her, no, screaming at her, that the events of that morning were just a bit off.

She felt an almost desperate desire to call Don. At the very least, he would reassure her that she had an overactive imagination and that everything was exactly as it seemed. At the very worst, well, she didn't want to think about what that very worst might be.

She walked past the lobby bar and glanced at where she and Don had first met, half hoping to see him standing there with his warm smile and alluring sapphire eyes, but since it was Sunday morning, the bar was closed.

As soon as she entered her room Melanie latched the door behind her. She found her cell phone and called her voice mail to check her messages. Thankfully, there was only one from the producer saying that rehearsals were on schedule, he hoped she had a good reunion, and the cast and crew couldn't wait to get started on the new season.

Melanie turned off the cell and put it on the coffee table, removed her sweatshirt and pants and carefully laid them over the back of the chair. Exhausted, she dragged herself to the bathroom, removed her bra and panties, opened the glass shower door and turned on the jet sprays.

She was just about to step into the welcoming waters when the wall phone rang. Whoever thought it was a good idea to put telephones in hotel bathrooms should be shot, she thought. She turned off the water and lifted the receiver, nearly pulling the entire phone off the wall. When she heard the voice on the other end, she instantly changed her opinion about the person who thought it was a good idea to install phones in bathroom.

"Hi Mel" Don said. "I was hoping to catch you before you left for the brunch. I'm glad you were in your hotel room. I tried your cell, but it went directly to your voice-mail."

"Sorry, the battery is getting low and I left my charger at home, so after I checked my messages I turned it off."

Really good thing there's a phone in the bathroom, she thought.

"I was hoping you'd call," She heard an uncomfortable long pause and thought he might have hung up.

"Don? You still there?"

"Sorry, I just woke up," he said.

"You just woke up?"

"Yeah, I'm not as young as I used to be," He joked. "All-nighters should be left to the young guys. Stu volunteered to head Wyatt's arrest later, so I'm taking the rest of the day off. We'll get a full de-briefing first thing tomorrow morning. As far as I'm concerned, the mission is over, and it was a complete success thanks to you and your girlfriend. I think you and I should celebrate over dinner."

For a moment, Melanie completely forgot about her earlier anxiety. Maybe her subconscious was only sending her signals that she wanted to spend more time with Don and nothing more.

"I was planning on going to the reunion brunch to say good-bye to anyone who may still be hanging around, so dinner would be perfect."

"Sounds like a plan," Don said. "Get some rest and I'll pick you up at seven."

Melanie felt his smile through the phone wires. Even though he was no where in the room, his voice made her entire body blush.

"Seven it is."

She returned the phone to the wall unit and once again turned the water on in the shower. The hot spray caressed her hair, its relaxing heat flowed over her body releasing all the tension of the previous days.

Her thoughts were not on UNCLE, or Wyatt, or the fact that she had just been released from a concrete prison, but on the handsome agent with the beautiful blues eyes and soft smile she would be dining with later that night.

Stepping out of the shower, Melanie put on the soft, complementary terry cloth robe, and wrapped a towel around her hair. She was about to open the bathroom door, when her hand froze on the knob. She could swear she heard muffled voices coming from the living room of her suite. Melanie turned the doorknob as quietly as possible and slowly opened the door just wide enough to see into the adjoining room, but from as far as she could tell, the room was empty.

Straining to hear any other sounds, she was relieved that the only noise in the room was coming from the air conditioner. She cautiously walked out of the bathroom, pausing every few steps to listen intently, but there were no other sounds coming from anywhere in the hotel suite.

"It's no wonder I'm a bit jumpy, after what I've just been through.

Melanie returned to the bathroom and, as she dried her skin, her mind replayed Don's soft, masculine tones asking her to dinner. A normal date, she thought. No spies, no undercover mission, just a really nice good looking man asking a talented, intelligent, and highly attractive lady out to dinner. Melanie turned on the hair drier, and put the brush to the wet strands.

She started to think what she was going to wear for her actual date, what she should say, what Don would say, when suddenly her hand suddenly stopped in mid-air as she recalled, word for word, the entire conversation.

Don hadn't mentioned the rescue at Wyatt's, or told her what happened to Eric and Charles.

Once again that uneasy feeling that something was just not right sent a shiver through her body. She turned off the hair dryer and was about to pick up the hotel phone to call him, when she remembered that she only had Stuart's card in her purse and had no idea how to get hold of Don.

"Damn," she said aloud to the empty room. "Don said they disconnected the communicator pen, but maybe the cigarette case's transmitter is still active."

Melanie went to the outer room to retrieve the case from her sweatshirt pocket, but when she walked over to the chair where she remembered putting it, she discovered the sweatshirt laying in a crumpled heap on the floor. Melanie knew she was over-tired, but even in her exhausted state, she was positive she wouldn't have been so careless. She picked up the sweatshirt and began searching the front pocket for the cigarette case and communicator pen, but the pocket was empty and both items were gone. She tried to recall if she had dropped them somewhere between the time they left Wyatt's and when she returned to her room, but nothing came to her.

She recalled that Don had told her he had tried to call her cell phone. Thinking his number would be on the voice-mail call list, she looked on the table where she had left it, but the cell phone was also gone. Melanie checked her purse, all of the drawers and under all of the furniture, but there was no sign of her phone, or the missing communication devices.

Holding onto the coffee table for balance, Melanie brought herself upright, in direct line of sight with the front door. What she saw caused her uneasy feeling to rise to the level of near panic.

The security latch was in the unlocked position.

Melanie stared at the door, her heart was pounding so hard it felt as if it would burst through her chest. The ringing of the hotel phone pierced the silence. Melanie literally jumped a full foot into the air.

Hoping it was Don calling to confirm the dinner date, she was disappointed to hear another man's voice instead.

"Mel? This is Stu. I just wanted to call and let you know that you left your cell phone at headquarters earlier, in case you were looking for it."

Stuart was lying to her. Melanie knew that she just used her phone to call her agent. She decided it was best to play dumb.

"Thanks, Stu. I thought I'd left it in my purse, but since I haven't had any reason to use it, I didn't notice it was missing. By the way, did I return my communicator pen to you or Don?"

"Yes, don't you remember? You handed it to me after we rescued you from Wyatt's. I was planning on going to the reunion brunch. I can bring your phone then."

In her calmest voice, which she did not feel at all, Melanie replied, "That would be great. I'll see you later."

All of Melanie's protective senses were instantly turned on full strength. She might be exhausted, but she knew damn well that she hadn't given Stuart the communicator pen or the cigarette case and she also knew she hadn't left her cell phone at UNCLE headquarters either.

As much as she needed to sleep, Melanie was running on pure adrenaline. She was determined to get much more than her cell phone from Stuart when they met at the brunch. She was going to get answers.

Chapter Twenty

As soon as he hung up the phone, Don wanted to call Melanie back and cancel their dinner. He didn't know what he was thinking. That was exactly the point, he wasn't thinking, just acting on his well-tuned instincts. There was something going on inside the agency and for the first time in his career, Don felt totally out of the loop.

In all previous missions, when he and Stuart had worked together, Don was always the lead agent. It wasn't that he was more capable, or more experienced than Stuart, it's just that Stuart never asserted himself on any assignment, preferring to be the back-up rather than the point man. Don thought it a bit odd that his partner had volunteered to take charge of Wyatt's arrest, and although busting Wyatt and all of THRUSH would have resulted in Don receiving huge commendations, if his friend and partner wanted to take some of the glory, Don was more than happy to let him.

After the success of the morning's operation all Stu really needed to do was the clean-up once everyone arrived at Wyatt's later that evening. Stuart would have plenty of back-up, and he was well trained, so when he asked Don if he could finish the assignment solo, Don didn't have any reason to argue. Besides, if Melanie was only going to be in town one more day, he would much rather spend his time with one beautiful woman than a smelly bunch of counterfeiters.

When he called Melanie's cell phone and the call went directly to voice mail, he became concerned, but when she answered her hotel phone and explained about her battery, he felt like an over-protective father hen. The awkward pause in the conversation hadn't helped any either.

Putting his trained agent's concerns aside, Don turned his thoughts to more pleasant matters. He still needed to take a shower and shave then check into headquarters and complete his reports before meeting Melanie for dinner. If things went well after dessert, he was also going to begin putting in his transfer request to the Los Angeles office.

Across town, Wyatt Gaynes was feeling better than he had in years. In just a few hours, his counterfeit Euros would begin to circulate throughout all the countries in the European Union, along with thousands of good ole Uncle Sam twenty dollar bills. Once James killed the anti-toxic dye bill, he was able to obtain the correct chemicals he needed.

The shipments of paper were being delivered through his underground aqueducts and the computers were programmed to start the presses as soon as they arrived. All the pieces of were in place. Decades of planning, of lies and manipulation, of blackmail and extortion, were about to come to fruition in a matter of hours.

Wyatt wished Melanie and Katie hadn't poked their noses into his business. He hated having to lock the women in the concrete room with his former accomplices, but that unfortunate state of things most probably saved all their lives. Wyatt hadn't planned on letting either Charles or Eric leave his employ alive. He couldn't take the risk that they would turn him in as soon as they had the chance, or would be potential witnesses against him should they get caught.

But he never expected that Katie or Melanie, especially Melanie, would be involved, or that they would be caught in his operation room as well. He was puzzled as to why there were there in the first place. They couldn't have been working with the men, but once he found them in his control room, he couldn't take any chances. He had no choice but to get them into the sound proof room where they wouldn't be able to hear the presses running. Wyatt was so close to success he couldn't take the chance of any one of them screwing up his plans. Even though he couldn't have cared less about the fate of the traitorous men, the women were just in the wrong place at the wrong time, so Wyatt felt he had to go back to the room and release them after his men had finished loading the freshly printed money onto the shipping platforms.

He'd been on his way to free his prisoners, but when he saw Stuart arrive, he decided to let him rescue the four. He had no idea how Stuart knew where his prisoners were being held. He had seen them all talking with Stuart at the reunion and it would not have surprised Wyatt in the slightest if either of the men had brought Stuart in on the sabotage, or that Stuart would have agreed to help them, especially after what Wyatt had done to him back in high school to get even for that damn Mr. Silver nickname.

Either way, there were way too many people getting in the way of Wyatt's final operation, so if Stuart could get everyone out of the way for awhile, that was just fine with him.

Wyatt watched Eric and Charles rush toward the exit. Then, he saw Melanie and Katie followed Stuart up the stairs. Once they were no longer in view, Wyatt returned to the underground aqueduct to wait for the THRUSH submarines that would take the counterfeit Euros to his international operation in Paris. Wyatt was confident that his over-seas contacts would be ready to accept the shipment since he had personally talked to each and every one of them that morning.

He had no regrets for all he had done to accomplish his goal. Except one. He'd never be able to forget the look of loathing that he had seen in Melanie's eyes when he closed the concrete door. He had hurt her back when they were in junior high, then right after graduation, and had used her to make his girlfriend jealous ten years after that.

Why, after all that, she had invited him to her room, he had no idea. He only wished he could have remembered their love making. Even though she told him how wonderful he had been, of that Wyatt had no doubt, he only wished he could have remembered the details. After putting her in that room with the others, he doubted that she would ever reveal the events of their passionate night, or, for that matter, ever speak to him again and he certainly deserved it if she didn't, but that was a problem for another day.

With his operation firmly in place and ready for the evening's events, Wyatt decided that he would attend the farewell reunion brunch if only to finally end any reference to that damn nick-name. After tonight, his classmates, and the entire world would be calling him Mr. Gold.

Chapter Twenty-One

By the time Melanie arrived at the brunch a good number of reunion guests had already returned to their homes and their twenty-first century lives. Even though it was almost over, she was glad she was able to spend a bit of normal time in Abbeyville with people she knew she'd never see again. Unfortunately, one of those people had also decided to make a final appearance. "I can't believe you would show your face here after what you tried to do to us this morning, Wyatt!"

It was all she could do not to slap his face, but that would lead to too many questions that she'd rather not answer.

"Mel, I didn't expect to see you here. I thought you were heading back to Los Angeles," Wyatt said, then in a whisper added, "You were in the wrong place at the wrong time. That's all. You know I'd never do anything to hurt you."

"The hell I do," She shot back. "That's all you've been doing since the day we met back in the sixth grade. After today, I never want to see or hear from you again, understand?"

Melanie turned and walked to the buffet table, but she had totally lost her appetite. She put a few items on her plate and decided to join in a few conversations that had nothing whatever to do with spies, hidden rooms, or Wyatt Gaynes.

For the first few minutes it seemed her wish had been granted. The divorced women were talking about their huge alimony checks, the grandparents were bragging about their grandkids, the guys were either talking about their successful business, or reliving their golden days playing high school football. The small talk might have interested her a few days ago, but in light of what she had just experienced, it was boring her to tears.

Oh, how she wanted to tell them! She couldn't even reveal what she actually did for a living let alone what she had been doing the past few days. They probably wouldn't have believed me anyway, she thought. Melanie was about to get a cup of coffee when she spotted one classmate she could talk to. Stuart had arrived, and along with him, her lost cell phone.

"There you are, Mel," he said, "and here's your cell. You getting ready to leave?"

Melanie took the phone from his hand.

"Yes. My flight leaves at five a.m. tomorrow, so I'm calling it an early night. I'm dead tired, but I thought I'd come to the brunch and say good-bye to whoever was still hanging around. Too bad Eric and Chuck are missing all the fun," She said sarcastically. "But, ya know, they don't seem to be missed."

"They're both spilling their guts back at UNCLE headquarters," Stuart said. "Look at Wyatt schmoozing with everyone as if he doesn't have a care in the world,"

Stu motioned to where Wyatt was laughing with a few of the women.

"That guy just never turns off the charm does he?"

"Nope, never. Even when it no longer works, he keeps trying. One of these days someone is going to turn it off for him."

"Not to worry. Once I get the arrest warrant, Wyatt won't be bothering you or me, or anyone else for a very long time. Thanks to you and Katie, I have everything in place to complete this assignment. "

"Don't you mean we? I'd hate to think you're going after Wyatt and his entire operation all by yourself," Melanie said.

"Did I say I? Guess I'm catching that bad habit from Wyatt. Speaking of the main man, it looks like he's getting ready to leave which is my cue to get out of here, too. Have a safe flight Mel, and thanks again."

Melanie purposely didn't mention her date with Don later that night. Now that their mission was over, she felt that her personal life really wasn't any of Stuart's concern, or perhaps she was feeling just a bit paranoid about exactly how her cell phone ended up in Stuart's hand.

She flipped open the case and checked her voice and text messages. They were all still there, including the emergency number for UNCLE headquarters, as well as all her entries in her address book and calendar. Everything appeared to be fine. Maybe it was just her over-active imagination, or perhaps she was becoming a bit too involved with her pseudo-spy role. As an actor, the lines between reality and fantasy often became so blurred, it was difficult to tell the difference.

She also wondered if Don was also playing a role, and his interaction with her was just the way the performed on all his assignment. There was only way to find out, Melanie thought. Instead of playing some childish high school game of manipulation and subtle hints, she was going to be an adult and simply ask him.

Melanie made her way down to the lobby for the final farewell to her less than stellar past and, if everything worked out as she planned, a much more pleasant future.

Chapter Twenty-Two

The last few members of the class of '72 said their good-byes, exchanged e-mail addresses and made promises to keep in touch that none of them intended to keep. The pleasantries were as phony and the promises as empty as the end-of-high-school greetings each had scrawled to one another over their yearbook photographs thirty years ago.

Everyone had been so very happy to see Stuart at the reunion. No one seemed to remember that they never signed his yearbook, or question why he hadn't graduated with the rest of the class. Those that did were too polite to ask, and Stuart wasn't about to satisfy their curiosity, not now, not ever. It was enough that he had returned to his hometown with a mission to finish. A mission that had begun long before he joined UNCLE

Stuart got into his car and waited until he saw Wyatt pull out of the parking lot before starting the engine. Keeping at a safe distance, he followed the black Mercedes as it proceeded through the streets of Abbeyville. As expected, Wyatt was on his way back to his base of operations with Stuart right on his tail.

It might have been UNCLE's mission to thwart Wyatt's international counterfeiting plan, it had been Stuart's goal to do a lot more to his old friend for what Wyatt had done to him over thirty years ago. Even now, Stuart could feel his stomach tighten to the point of becoming nauseous. He forced himself to keep the digested brunch salads from making a return appearance as he followed Wyatt's car. The streets of Abbeyville looked entirely different then when the very young, very naive Stuart Janns had left town under the cover of darkness the summer before his senior year.

In the more enlightened twenty-first century, having a gay son or daughter was not nearly as devastating to a family as it was in decades past. Back then it was a great deal easier and safer to stay hidden in the closet. Since his early teens, Stuart had known he was different from the other boys in his class, but in a small town, with even smaller minds, even the slightest rumor of homosexuality would destroy a young teenager's life.

In the late sixties, there were no organized gay pride events and no support groups for parents of gay children. The only other gay classmate Stuart knew was literally thrown out into the street after he had told his parents. Even though he felt his family would never resort to such drastic measures, they were solid church going members of the community and the scandal alone might have changed their minds. So, he had kept his secret well hidden for years. Until he made the mistake of confiding in his best friend, Wyatt Gaynes.

Stuart recalled the details of that faithful night as if it had occurred only yesterday. It was the end of summer before their Senior year when he, Wyatt, Eric, Charles, and several other boys had gone camping at the lake to celebrate one of their last nights of freedom before school resumed. They were sitting around the campfire talking about sports and girls, and the sport of girls. Stuart tried to fake interest, but he was more uncomfortable than anything else, so he'd made the excuse that he was tired and headed back toward his tent. A few minutes later Wyatt, saying he was concerned that Stuart wasn't feeling well, followed him and asked what was wrong.

Maybe it had been the sincerity in his voice, or the fact that Stuart just had a desperate need to confide in someone. For whatever reason, Stuart came out of the tent, and the closet, and had told Wyatt everything that night. At first, his friend hadn't said anything. Stuart didn't know if Wyatt was in shock or just too frightened to speak, but after the first few awkward seconds of silence, Wyatt appeared to completely understand. He told Stuart that it didn't matter, he was still his friend and no matter what, Stuart could always come to him anytime to talk or just hang out.

For a moment, for a very brief moment, Stuart felt as if a huge weight he'd been carrying around for years had finally been lifted from his shoulders.

He'd asked Wyatt not to tell anyone, and Wyatt swore to him that he wouldn't. Wyatt had told Stuart that he was glad he'd valued their friendship so highly that he would trust him with his deepest secret. Then he'd left. For the first time in a very long time, Stuart had gotten a good night's sleep. It wasn't until the next morning he discovered that his worst nightmare had come true.

When he joined them for breakfast, he noticed his friends acting strangely. They moved away from him when he walked over to the picnic table, and not one of them would look him in the eye. Then, the teasing began.

Eric offered Stuart "fruit", and Charles pretended to cough the word "fag" into his hands, but pretty soon it became quite obvious that Wyatt had outed him to everyone in the group. Stuart tried to play along and take it as a really bad joke, but after a few minutes of homo-jokes, he was fed up. He ran back to his tent, packed up his belongings and drove home.

The sound of the boy's taunts, and Wyatt's laughter had followed him all the way to his house. He knew that it wouldn't be long before his secret was all over town, and Stuart had no choice but to talk to his parents, who, much to his relief, were a great deal more enlightened then he thought. Instead of forcing him from their home, they suggested, and he agreed, that he move to New York City to live with his aunt and finish his education in a more anonymous city.

Even though he was miles from home, Stuart found life in the Big Apple to be as exciting as he'd heard, and a far cry from the closed-minds who lived in Abbeyville, Minnesota. He graduated top of his class and was accepted to Columbia, where he began writing theater reviews for the college paper. He was approached by an UNCLE recruiter shortly after graduation. With the allure of international travel and total acceptance of his sexual identity, Stuart had enthusiastically accepted. In a way, he had Wyatt to thank for his successful new career, but he never forgot the pain and humiliation he had suffered that night because of Wyatt Gaynes.

When UNCLE first began to be suspicious of Wyatt's activities, Stuart immediately volunteered to join the task force and proceeded to follow Wyatt's trail in cities across Europe, while sending reviews back to NewsTime magazine, and reports to UNCLE headquarters.

Stuart's professional life was going extremely well, but his personal life was going nowhere, until he met Francois in a Paris café. He was funny and sensitive and it hadn't taken Stuart long to succumb to his attention and affection.

Francois was a successful fashion designer who introduced Stuart to some of the finest elite in the Paris art world. Although he didn't think very much of Francois' style of haute couture, he was totally enthralled with the designer and his lifestyle. It wasn't long before the boy from Minnesota was sipping Cristal and eating Beluga caviar with the best of them, but he also realized that his new lifestyle was only due to his relationship with Francois, and it could vanish in an instant if Francois found someone else to share his bed.

The direction of Stuart Janns' life changed drastically one cold night when he was covering the Cannes Film Festival. He was also on assignment for UNCLE doing surveillance on Wyatt when he was approached by Pierre, who introduced himself as a client of Francois. At first, Stuart had thought Pierre was simply trying to get an invitation to Francois' runway show where he was going to introduce his new line. As it turned out, the line he was after was attached to a very tempting bait for Stuart.

On the last night of fashion week, Pierre invited Stuart to his suite and, in a line from an old movie, made him an offer that he couldn't refuse. Pierre revealed that he was working with a group of business men who were organizing a counterfeiting operation with a guy in the states, whose family owned a paper mill, Stuart was immediately hooked. All he had to do was provide Pierre with information on Wyatt's activities, and keep that information from the authorities in the U.S. For his service, he was promised that he would be discreetly rewarded.

It wasn't any secret that UNCLE didn't pay their agents anywhere near the salary Stuart needed to ensure that he could continue with his lifestyle by himself if anything should happen to his lover. Stuart convinced himself that he really wasn't doing anything wrong by withholding information from his UNCLE contacts, and the money was just too good to pass up, and if that meant working against Wyatt Gaynes, that was just a very nice perk.

So began Stuart's life as a double agent. Even Don hadn't suspected anything, but as Stuart became more and more involved with the European cartel, it wasn't enough for him to simply provide information on Wyatt to Pierre, or help UNCLE bring him to justice. Stuart began formulate a plan to take over Wyatt's entire operation. And that plan would go into high gear during the weekend of their thirtieth high school reunion. On the very night that Wyatt believed he was going to have it all, Stuart would be the one to take it all from him, and he would do it right in front of Wyatt's accomplices. Stuart had waited more than thirty years to pay Wyatt back for what he had done to him on that camping trip, and as they say, payback is a real bitch.

What Stuart hadn't counted on, however, was one very intelligent and very loyal UNCLE agent named Donald Wagner.

On a typical Sunday, the Abbeyville UNCLE headquarters was usually empty. Unlike those in larger cities, which operated round-the-clock, nothing extraordinary ever warranted overtime. Today was different. It wasn't that Don was checking up on Stuart, he would have performed his professional duties regardless, so no one thought anything of Don coming into work on what would have normally been his day off. After making dinner plans with Melanie, he wanted to spend his free hours making certain that the operation would run smoothly so he wouldn't have it on his mind when he met her. The only "affair" he wanted to concentrate on was the one he hoped to have with the lovely lady from L.A.

As expected, there was a huge stack of files waiting for him on his desk. Don poured himself a cup of coffee to push the last bit of sleep from his eyes and began reading.

"What the hell?" he said aloud when he read the first page on top of the file.

In what looked like his handwriting was a report on a rescue operation that had occurred that morning. The incident involved Melanie, Katie, Charles and Eric, and gave great detail about him arresting the men after they had tried to run. The only problem was that Don was sleeping at the time of their supposed arrest and he hadn't filled out any report.

He picked up the phone and entered Melanie's cell phone number. Before the call connected, he heard a loud buzz, indicating that the number he was calling was being tapped. The call was immediately intercepted before it could connect. He tried calling Stuart, but received a message that the number was no longer working.

Don was becoming more concerned. He put in a call to the Minneapolis office to see if there had been any reports of a rescue, or the arrest of Charles and Eric. He was told that yes, they had received his fax and they were very pleased with the way he had handled the operation. They were very impressed with his very detailed report. It was exceptional work, they'd said, especially since he had a reputation for being a bit sloppy with such things in the past.

The secretary joked that maybe the Midwest small town work ethic was starting to rub off on him. Don was about to correct her, when he remembered there was an agent he knew who was obsessed with details on every report he filed. Stuart had always chastised Don for procrastinating on the paperwork, and had, several times in the past, filed the reports for Don, even perfecting his signature.

Don opened the file cabinet and pulled out the last report that Stuart had filed for him, and compared it with the one he found on his desk. There was no doubt that the style was Stuart's, even though it would take a handwriting expert to see the subtle difference between Don's signature and that of the forgery.

An all too familiar feeling was beginning to creep inside Don's gut. It was the nauseous feeling that someone he trusted, with his very life, was going to betray him.

For some in the business of law enforcement, it sometimes takes only a tiny step off the straight and narrow to lead to a much deeper fall, Don thought.

Over the years, he'd seen only a few good, trusted agents fall prey to their own human weaknesses. Carla Drosten, former head of Section 6 was one who nearly got away with it. Harry Beldon, another high ranking agent had been responsible for the total destruction of their Geneva headquarters. Many good agents died as a result of their actions for reasons known only to those who chose the destiny. Don wondered what it was that had made his trusted friend take that first fatal step. Sometimes the reason was just burn-out with the long hours, low pay, and little reward, but the reason, more often than not, was basic human greed.

Under normal circumstances, agents would never run a financial check on another agent's accounts. Out in the field, the only thing that meant the difference between life and death was the protection one had from a partner of unquestionable trust. New agents were tested in a number of ways, and each received intense evaluations, especially after every mission, but even UNCLE's best techniques were not perfect and occasionally they were dead wrong. But never once, in all his experience, was the dirty agent his partner.

Maybe he was getting old, or maybe he was just becoming too complacent with the Midwestern lifestyle, but Don was furious with himself for not seeing what Stuart was up to sooner.

Although he had taken every security precaution to cover his tracks, Don was able to access Stuart's overseas accounts. There were several large international transactions into and out of Stuart's account, and more than a few to a stationery store on Main Street.

Don didn't know what connection, if any, Stuart had with Wyatt Gaynes, but it was too late to try and expose him. That would have to wait until after they arrested Wyatt. Don couldn't risk having five years of planning go to hell, and there would be plenty of time to bring Stuart in, after he completed his assignment. Don also had to find out what happened to Eric and Charles, and somehow accomplish it all before his dinner date with Melanie.

Don knew he was a good agent, but at his age, he wasn't quite sure he was that good anymore.

Chapter Twenty-Three

Melanie said her final good-byes to the remaining classmates and returned to her room. She was relieved that Wyatt had left before her. As far as she was concerned, her last good-bye to Wyatt was definitely her last and final good-bye.

Her date with Don wasn't for another few hours, so Melanie decided that now would be a good time to catch up on some much needed rest. This time, she made certain that both the safety bolt and the chain link latch were secure.

With so much on her mind, Melanie didn't think she would be able to sleep, but she was out the moment her head hit the pillow. Her dreams were a mixture of Wyatt back in high school, Wyatt's hand holding a gun to her face, Wyatt turning into a fire breathing dragon, and then Don riding in on a white horse to slay the dragon and rescue the maiden in distress. She woke up just as the dream had them riding off into the sunset. She laughed aloud at the way her mind put her into so many scenes she had read in scripts, but not one of them ever had become part of her reality, until this weekend.

Melanie washed her face, put on fresh make-up and put on an outfit that she thought would be perfect for a casual dinner date with a handsome, mysterious man. The powder-blue blouse brought out the gold specks in her eyes and accented the highlights in her hair. Matched with a pair of light gray pants, and beige sandals she was definitely not the typical Minnesotan, not by a long shot. She was finally beginning to feel like the successful, professional actor she thought she had left in Los Angeles and was looking forward to a nice, relaxing dinner, some intelligent conversation, and perhaps a bit more after dessert if things went well.

Maybe it was the high school atmosphere the past few days, or the fact that she hadn't had a real date in years, but Melanie was overcome with first-date jitters. The hotel bar had re-opened for the Sunday evening after-dinner crowd, and even though it was only six-thirty, Melanie thought a quick drink before her date with Don would quiet her nerves.

She left her room and headed toward the elevator when she noticed several men milling in the hallway waiting for the elevator doors to open. She could hear them talking, but from her distance, couldn't make out what they were saying. As she approached, she realized they were speaking French and she understood every word. She smiled politely at the men and they returned the greeting briefly. Assuming Melanie couldn't understand their conversation, they continued talking.

"Vous êtes certain il n'a pas ce qui se passe?" one asked.

You're certain he has no idea what's going on?

"Notre contact nous a assurés qu'il pense que nous rencontrerons pour signer l'affaire. Le temps il chiffre nous reprenons son opération, Wyatt Gaynes sera mort," The other replied.

Our contact has assured us that he thinks we're going to be meeting to sign the deal. By the time he figures out we're taking over his operation, Wyatt Gaynes will be dead.

Melanie didn't need to translate the name of their target, Wyatt's name was the same in any language. Using all her acting skills to calm herself, she exited the elevator and slowly walked around the corner where she could keep an eye on the men, but they wouldn't be able to see her.

Melanie wished more than ever that Don had given her his direct phone number, but all she had was the agency's main number she had saved on speed dial. Doing her best to keep her hand steady while keeping an eye on the increasing number of hit men amassing in the lobby, she opened her cell phone and pressed the keypad.

Expecting to hear the voice of a receptionist, Melanie was surprised to hear Stuart's instead. She didn't have any time to ask him why. She repeated, word for word in English, what she had overheard, then waited for Stuart to respond. When he did, she was relieved to hear him reassure her in a very calm and soothing manner.

"Thanks for the heads-up, Mel. I'll call Don, assemble a team and we'll get over to Wyatt's. It shouldn't take more than thirty minutes."

"Stu, I don't know if Wyatt has thirty minutes!" Melanie's panic was obvious. "Look, if I leave now and take the side streets, I can be there in ten."

"YOU STAY RIGHT WHERE YOU ARE! We've been working this operation for years and we're not about to allow anyone to screw it up!"

Stuart was practically yelling, then his voice changed to a more soothing tone. "Sorry, Mel. But Wyatt and whoever is after him are far too dangerous and we don't want anything happening to you. Leave this to the professionals, ok?"

"Ok, Stu. You're probably right. Call me when it's over, please."

"Of course I will. Don't worry, Mel, Wyatt will be taken care of."

As soon as the call disconnected, Melanie opened her message list and hit the redial button next to Wyatt's name. If she couldn't warn him in person, she thought, at least she could call him. But when she tried to make the call, her phone showed a message that there was no signal. She tried it once more, but the message was the same.

Melanie glanced around the corner of the wall. She counted six men sitting around the lobby, talking as if nothing unusual was happening. None of them were paying any attention to the woman who was on her way to the hallway where the pay phones were located. She grabbed some change from her purse, and was about to put a few coins in the slot, but when she put the receiver to her ear, there wasn't any dial tone.

She tried all the other phones on the wall, but not one produced a dial tone. With all the advances in communication technology available, she thought, it was frustrating as hell that when I need one the most, not one of them worked!

Melanie began walking toward the reception desk, but before she was able to speak to one of the staff, another guest pushed in front of her.

"Why aren't any of the phones working?" he yelled. "I can't even access my wi-fi on my laptop and I have an important call coming in!"

The receptionist tried to calm him, but Melanie could tell that she was as upset about the situation as he was.

"I'm really sorry, sir, the entire system just went down a few minutes ago. We're trying to contact our IT Division, but as you just said, none of the phones or internet are working. I'm sure everything will be fine in a few minutes."

The receptionist didn't sound so sure.

Melanie was starting to become increasingly anxious. Even though Stuart had told her to stay at the hotel, she had to find out if the UNCLE operatives had managed to get to Wyatt's in time, and if not, she was going to warn him herself. As much as she hated Wyatt and as much as she wanted him to pay for everything he'd done to her, to James and Katie, and to everyone who had ever considered him a friend, she wanted him punished, she didn't want him dead.

If she left before the men in suits, she could get to Wyatt's and warn him before they arrived, she thought. And if she saw UNCLE agents already there, she'd keep on driving, but if there were no cars on the street, she was going to warn Wyatt no matter what Stuart had said about the operation. Maybe it would completely foul up years of work that went into planning Wyatt's arrest, and she might be walking into a very dangerous situation, she was willing to take that chance. Even though she wasn't sure that, if the roles were reversed, Wyatt would have done the same for her.

Melanie wished more then ever that she hadn't returned the revolver to Don, but she was confident that Stuart and his agents would either be there before she arrived, or shortly after to back her up if anything went wrong. She only had to time it right and get to Wyatt's before everyone else arrived.

Although they didn't seem to be in any hurry, Melanie noticed the men starting to move toward the exit. She was very relieved that none of them noticed her walking through the doorway ahead of them.

As soon as Melanie cleared the parking lot, she hit the gas and tore through the Sunday streets of Abbeyville. Melanie pulled up to Wyatt's in just under eight minutes. She hit the brakes and the car came to a screeching halt directly in front of the alley between Wyatt's stores. She looked up one side of the street and down the other, but didn't see a single automobile or a living body. There might have been surveillance from any of the other surrounding stores, but the sidewalks were empty of any life. On one hand, Melanie thought, that was a good thing, because it meant that no one else was inside with Wyatt. On the other hand, it wasn't such a good thing because if meant that Stuart and the UNCLE agents hadn't yet arrived.

Melanie knew she was taking a huge risk, but for the sake of their very long friendship, and perhaps for the "what might have been" if their lives had taken different paths, she knew she had to warn Wyatt. Melanie took a deep breath, left her car, walked into the alley and through the door where she had escaped from only hours, which now felt like years, ago.

Chapter Twenty-Four

Melanie entered her birthday code into the touch pad on the side of the door leading to the Wyatt's base of operations. She cautiously removed her heels, so her footsteps wouldn't make any sound just in case he wasn't alone. She found him in the control room, his back toward her. He was talking on the phone and didn't hear her enter. Once she noticed that he was alone, she began to run toward him. Startled, Wyatt grabbed his gun, but when he saw who it was, put it back in his holster and put his finger to his lips in a motion to signal her to be quiet, then motioned that he'd be off the phone in a second.

"Mel? What on earth are you doing here?" he asked when the call ended. "I didn't think I'd ever see you again after what you said at the brunch. I guess I was right about us."

"Wyatt, listen to me!" Melanie yelled, "This has nothing to do with us, or not us. DAMMIT, Wyatt there is no us!"

Ignoring her, Wyatt moved to pick up the phone.

"Mel, as much as I'm glad to see you, I really have a very important meeting in about a half hour..."

Melanie put her finger on the phone base, cutting him off.

"Wyatt, that's why I'm here. You have to listen to me. I know about the meeting. These guys at the hotel, they were speaking French and didn't know I could understand what they were saying."

"I always knew you were smart, Mel," Wyatt was amused.

"Wyatt, cut it out. I'm serious. I overheard them saying they were going to kill you at this meeting. You have to get out of here before they arrive."

"Melanie, you told me they were speaking a different language. You probably just mis-understood. I've been working with those men for years, they know they couldn't put this deal together without me. I'm the mastermind of this operation."

"Wyatt, I know you think you're the master of something other than your own domain, but I'm telling you, I'm quite fluent in French and I did not mis-understand anything. Even if I did, there's something else that I have to tell you, like the reason I know what you're up to."

Wyatt was becoming annoyed with Melanie's crazy accusations. He knew she didn't know anything of the kind, but still it didn't hurt to ask.

"Oh really? And what would that be?"

Before she had a chance to answer, Stuart came running into the room with four other men, their weapons pointing directly at Wyatt. Melanie was relieved that their entrance had stopped her from revealing to Wyatt that UNCLE was about to arrest him, or how it was that she knew that information. She was so glad to see Stuart, she was about to rush over to give him a hug when she noticed that the men who had accompanied him weren't the UNCLE agents she has met that morning, but the very men she'd seen in the elevator, who she had overheard threatening Wyatt's life.

"Stu? What are you doing with these guys?"

And where is Don and the other UNCLE agents?

Stuart ignored her question and instead turned his attention, and the barrel of his .45, onto Wyatt.

"Sorry to have to tell you this Wyatt, but you're no longer in control of THRUSH. Now, slowly put your gun on the console and move away from Melanie. Mel, I can't have you trying to contact the authorities, so please put your cell phone on the console, too."

"Stuart, what on earth are you doing?"

Melanie felt as if she were in a very bad dream, as she realized that her previous suspicions had, in fact, been correct. She was relieved, however, that Stuart hadn't revealed her involvement with UNCLE which would have most likely put her on the wrong side of both the THRUSH agents and Wyatt's weapons.

"Yea, Stuart, what the hell are you doing?"

Wyatt removed the gun from his holster and put it on the console next to Melanie's, but didn't move more than a few steps away from her side.

"It's very simple, Wyatt. Over the past several years while you thought you were reorganizing THRUSH, in reality you were only doing exactly what I wanted. All of your international contacts have been arrested by UNCLE and replaced by my operatives."

Melanie was in shock. Stuart Janns, the shy movie critic and Don's trusted partner a double agent?

"But you rescued us this morning and you told me that your partner arrested Eric and Charles."

Melanie was being very careful not to mention Don's name, or that she knew anything about UNCLE As far as Wyatt knew, she had only overheard a threatening conversation and was there to warn him. She wasn't quite sure how he would react if he knew that she had been working with Stuart and UNCLE the whole time.

"I lied. No one else knew anything about the rescue. I wrote up the reports with forged signatures, been doing it for years. I also broke into your hotel room to get your cell phone."

"That was you in my room? I don't believe this."

Melanie's fears were being replaced by sheer anger. She was half-tempted to pick up Wyatt's gun and shoot Stuart herself.

"Yes, I was hiding in the back closet when you arrived and once you went into the shower, I grabbed it and left. Then, before I returned it to you at the banquet I replaced the SIM card, so that any emergency calls you made would only go to me. I couldn't have you calling the local police and have those Keystone Cops totally screw up my plans, could I?"

Does everyone from our class have some kind of international plan? Melanie said under her breath. Then, to Stuart she said, "So it wasn't any coincidence that I called you, then my service died and I couldn't call anyone else."

One of the men answered. "Of course you couldn't. Our THRUSH agents shut down all communications right after you spoke to Janns. We couldn't have you phone Gaynes and warn him."

"I told you not to leave the hotel, Mel. I thought you were smarter than that. At the very least I didn't think you cared enough about Wyatt to risk you life to try and save him."

"Guess you were wrong, there, Stewy,"

Wyatt slowly began moving his hand towards the console, while keeping Stuart distracted. Sensing what Wyatt was trying to do, Melanie backed up a few steps.

"Well, you know how it is with old friends and former lovers. I guess I just never did manage to get Wyatt out of my system."

Melanie took a few steps backward to shield Wyatt's She could feel his nervous breath on her neck as she tried to keep Stuart and the other men distracted long enough for Wyatt to get his gun. She knew they were both taking a very big chance. The five-to-one odds of their getting out alive were very slim. If she kept Stuart talking, maybe hat would give Wyatt a bit more time to come up with a plan to get them out of danger.

"What happened to Eric and Chuck?"

"After the four of you came out of Wyatt's concrete room this morning, they disappeared as soon as they saw there wasn't anyone waiting for them on the other side of the door. My guess is that both of them are long gone but they're not my biggest problem at the moment. Mel, I'm sorry, you should have listened to me and stayed at the hotel. We only came to take care of Wyatt, but now I'm afraid you're going to have to come with us, too."

Stuart began walking toward Melanie and Wyatt. Melanie's gaze went through the men holding the guns and willed Don to burst through the door with the calvary, but no one came. She looked around for another way out of the control room and noticed there was a door directly behind Wyatt, but Stuart and the other four THRUSH agents still had their guns pointed right at them. Stuart took hold of Melanie's arm and started pulling her away from Wyatt.

"Stuart, you're never going to get away with this. I know too many people," Wyatt started to say.

"And everyone you know now works for me and the rest I'm sure aren't going to miss you. In fact I'm certain that most of them will be glad you're gone. Now, we're going to join the rest of my team at the loading dock below. Once we're gone, we'll blow this place and all that will be left of you two will be some very dirty ashes."

Stuart turned his head to Melanie and whispered, "I'm going to release your arm. I want you to run as fast as you can through that door behind you and get out of here. Don't worry, I'll cover you."

Melanie felt Stuart's grip on her ease a bit but just as she was about to make her escape, Wyatt pushed her to the floor, grabbed the gun from the console and fired at the armed assailants. Thinking she might still be able to make it to the back door, Melanie crawled a few inches, but bullets were flying everywhere, so instead she stayed crouched underneath the desk and hoped, as strange as it now seemed to say, that Wyatt would be able to rescue her.

How quickly things change, she thought. This morning she'd though that Stuart had rescued her from Wyatt, and now she was hoping that Wyatt would rescue her from Stuart.

A cold silence suddenly permeated the room. Melanie peered out from under the console to see if it was safe. A scant moment later, a familiar hand appeared.

"C'mon Mel," Wyatt said. "The coast, as they say, is clear. Let's get you out of here."

Melanie took Wyatt's hand and rose from her hiding place. Then, she saw that Wyatt was holding his gun in the other hand, and it was pointed at the still-standing Stuart. Scanning the room, she also noticed, the other four men slumped over in various positions on the floor. Splatters of blood covered most of the desk chairs, walls the even the ceiling.

Melanie was a bit surprised that neither Stuart nor Wyatt had any signs of injury, although with the two of them pointing a gun at the other, she was afraid that situation was going to change.

"I should kill you right now," Wyatt said, "Let the police find your dead body along with your friend's here," Wyatt spat out the words.

"You could do that Wyatt, but I have at least thirty more of my men on their way here. What do you think they'll do to Melanie? She's an innocent bystander in all of this, and an eye witness. Do you think they're just going to let her walk out of here?"

"Yeah, Wyatt, what about me?"

Melanie wasn't certain what Stuart or Wyatt's next plans were, either with her, or without her. But she was painfully aware that, at any moment, either of her two former classmates could very easily turn their weapons on her. She help her breath and waited for one of them to speak. Fortunately, Stuart spoke first.

"So, as much as I'm sure you want to pull that trigger, as much as I do, if you shoot me, who will tell my men that you were killed in the gunfire and I tossed your body down the elevator shaft, so you can make your escape?"

Melanie held her breath as the two men played chicken with their weapons. Finally, Wyatt returned his gun to his holster.

"You're probably right this time, Stuart but if I ever see you again..." Wyatt started.

"I know, you'll kill me. I got that. Now get out of here, both of you."

Chapter Twenty-Five

Wyatt, took hold of Melanie's hand and the two started moving toward the rear exit. With their backs turned they didn't see one of the wounded THRUSH agents lift his arm off the floor, pick up a gun and aim it directly at Melanie's back.

With no time to warn her, Stuart jumped in-between the bullet and its intended target. Wyatt pulled out his weapon and got off one more shot, ending the threat of the wounded assailant right after the bullet entered Stuart's solar plexus.

"Stuart, NO!"

Melanie screamed and ran to where Stuart had fallen. His shirt was already covered with a deep red stain that was growing larger by the second. Knowing he didn't have more than a few moments of life, Stuart reached into his shirt pocket and handed Melanie his communicator pen.

"It's working now," he coughed slightly. "Call Don. And tell him I'm sorry."

Melanie took the pen from Stuart. Her tears streamed down her face, landing on Stuart's lifeless body. Wyatt grabbed her arm and pulled her to her feet.

"Mel, come on, we've got to get out of here!"

Wyatt yelled over the sound of gunfire hitting the front door as the other THRUSH agents tried to enter the room. Melanie followed Wyatt through the doorway and into the elevator leading down to the aqueduct. Once they arrived, Wyatt immediately hit the electronic lock and grabbed a remote control from the shelf. He aimed the remote at one of the submarines, pressed the button and unlocked the latch.

"Go, get in. There's something I need to do before we leave."

As instructed, Melanie ran toward the sub, opened hatch and climbed into the cramped compartment. She wiped Stuart's blood from the communicator pen, hit the signal button and breathed a quiet sign of relief when she saw the green indicator light flash. She only hoped the signal was strong enough to get through the reinforced walls and UNCLE's communications satellite would be able to trace the signal underwater once she and Wyatt were on their way.

After what seemed like hours, Wyatt finally joined her in the cramped mini- sub. Without saying a word, he closed and locked the hatch. Then, he went over to the control pane and tuned on the engines.

"Where are we going?" she shouted over the noise.

"This aqueduct runs into Lake Superior. I have a seaplane waiting for us on Isle Royale that will fly you back to Abbeyville Lake." Wyatt yelled in reply.

"And what about you?"

"Don't worry about me, Mel. After I drop you off, I'll take the sub into Canada and disappear. I'm sure I still have a few loyal friends left on the other side of the border who owe me favors. You'd better sit down and strap yourself in, it's going to be a bumpy ride."

Melanie sat on one of the sub's benches and connected the lap belt and shoulder harness. As they began to submerge, the sea water covered the windows, making the cramped space feel even smaller in the dim interior light. She tried to calm her nerves with some deep breathing techniques she'd learned in acting class, but she couldn't shake her growing fear.

"What were you doing before we left?"

Melanie wasn't quite certain she wanted to know the answer, but before Wyatt could reply, the sub was hit by a shock wave from behind.

"That's what I was doing before we left. What you just heard was the sound of twenty years and several million dollars of hard work and planning going up in flames."

"Why on earth would you do that? Was anyone hurt?"

I hope that there were no UNCLE agents were in that room, thought Melanie. Especially not Don.

He answered her second question first

"I didn't see anyone else in the room when I set the charges, but I'm not going to shed any tears if those traitorous THRUSH bastards who were trying to kill me were caught in the explosion."

Wyatt checked some instruments before answering the other part of Melanie's question.

"Now that UNCLE has me in their sights, I needed to destroy any evidence of my operation, and any witnesses."

Melanie felt a sudden chill when she realized that Wyatt might have been talking about her. He tried to relieve her fears, but his next sentence had the opposite effect.

"Don't worry, Mel. You're safe. It's not like you're a Fed or anything, right?"

Melanie wasn't sure if Wyatt knew about her involvement with UNCLE and was toying with her but she wasn't going to reveal anything until she was safely back on dry land.

"Me? Don't be ridiculous Wyatt. I'm just an out-of-work actress. You know that."

She hoped he believed her. There wasn't any amount of seduction ploy that was going to save her if Wyatt discovered the truth. Before he could question her further, she turned the conversation to a topic she knew he would be much more interested in talking about; himself.

"Wyatt, tell me, how exactly did you get here?"

"We were being chased by a couple of thugs as I recall," he replied.

She slapped him on the thigh.

"You know that's not what I meant. How does a kid from a small town in Minnesota end up running for his life from both sides of the law?"

"Oh, that. Let's just say it was a series of unfortunate events that began a very long time ago. I trusted the wrong people, my father, my brother and Brenda to name a few. No one ever gave me a break. I took some very bad advice from some very stupid people and made choices that turned out to be the wrong ones."

Some things never change, thought Melanie. Wyatt had never taken responsibility for one damn thing his entire life, and it looked as if the trend was continuing.

"How could I know that Stuart Janns was going to turn my own people against me? Wasn't my fault he got himself killed. Speaking of Stuart, you should take that blouse off."

Wyatt reached for a blanket that was on an overhead shelf and handed it to Melanie.

"Here, put this on."

With all the anxiety about their precarious situation, Melanie hadn't notice her blouse, which she had so carefully selected for her date with Don, was covered in dark red blood stains.

"Thanks."

Melanie started to unbutton her blouse. She was painfully aware that Wyatt was watching her every move. Aware that she needed to move the communicator pen from her blouse, she asked,

"How much longer until we reach land?" Melanie asked, hoping to distract Wyatt long enough for her to hid the communicator pen. The ruse worked.

"Shouldn't be much longer. Let me check."

As soon as he turned his head to the control panel, she managed to put the pen in her pants pocket, then put the blanket over her shoulders. She didn't have a chance to check and see if the signal was still working and only hope that Don, or someone at the agency had received it. Wyatt turned back and answered her question.

"About an hour at this speed," he said. "Any faster and we might alert anyone watching for water disturbance. You look great, Mel, even in a blanket. I wish I could remember what happened last night."

"Isn't it enough that I remember, Wyatt?"

Melanie's voice was dripping with sexuality, then she changed tones to ask him the one question she'd been waiting a very long time him to answer. It was difficult, but she managed to get it all out in one sentence.

"And while we're on the subject of remembering, I know it's been thirty years and it really shouldn't matter to me this late in my life, and excuse me for sounding like a naive teenager, but exactly why didn't you call me after graduation?"

"Oh, that."

"Yes, that. Not a phone call, not a letter, nothing."

"The reason I didn't call you was because I knew you were leaving for California."

"Yeah, so?"

"People always leave. First my mom..."

"Wyatt, your mother died, it wasn't your fault."

"Sure it was, at least that's what my father always told me. He told everyone in town that my mother had accidently drowned trying to save me from falling into the lake, but the truth was that after she had me, she suffered from severe postpartum depression and eventually committed suicide. My father never said it out loud, but I know he blamed me for her death. He made me feel as if it was my fault for being born."

"Then he left me by spending so much time at work, or with Jack, his favorite. Then my high school girlfriend Terrie left me when she heard about that note you wrote, even though I told her I had nothing to do with it, and that any romantic involvement she thought you and I had was all in her imagination, but she didn't buy it. I knew that you were leaving, too and I wasn't about to take the chance of getting hurt again by someone I cared about, so this time, I left first."

Wyatt's explanation wasn't exactly what Melanie was expecting to hear. She was stunned by his story about his mother's suicide, and how Terrie had over reacted, but after everything that had happened, she wasn't sure she believed him, even now.

"You're saying that you actually cared about me? You certainly had a strange way of showing it. It that why you were all over me at James and Katie's anniversary party?"

"Partly. Brenda hurt me badly and I was trying to get even, but once you and I made love, everything changed. I knew that it really was you that wanted. I was going to explain everything to you later that night, but when I went back to the room, but you'd already left. I knew you were angry with me, and I'm really sorry for what happened. I only hope that I can make it up to you, starting right now."

Wyatt moved next to Melanie and put his arms around her.

"I never stopped thinking about you, Mel. Not once in all these years."

Leaning closer, Wyatt placed his hands on both sides of her face and brought her lips up to meet his. Just as he was about to kiss her, she put her hand up in front of his face. After years of voicing several fictional lives, Melanie knew a well rehearsed monologue when she heard it.

"Wyatt, does that line actually work for you?" she said.

"To tell you the truth, most of the time it does," Wyatt's grin made her laugh.

"I think that's the very first honest thing you've said to me since we got into this sub."

Melanie felt her body relax with the light hearted banter she was sharing with her sub-mate. Suddenly, alarm bells began blaring accompanied by red flashing lights that lit up the interior of tiny sub.

"What's that?" Melanie exclaimed.

Wyatt jumped over to where he'd been previously sitting and looked at the controls.

"I'm not sure, but from the look of the radar, it appears we're being followed. I guess those guys were able to get out of the aqueduct after all. From the speed they're going it appears that they're pretty pissed that I blew up their entire operation."

"Can we out-run them?"

Melanie was starting to panic.

"We got a good head start, but these mini-subs were only designed for short trips underwater to bring people and cargo from my place to a larger ship. We're going to have to surface or else they're going to catch us."

Melanie looked out the tiny window as the water level began to drop. Even though the sun had already set, it was still brighter on the surface and just seeing some light enter through the windows made her feel a bit more relaxed, until she heard a loud banging on the top of the mini-sub and a man's voice ordering Wyatt to open the hatch.

Chapter Twenty-Six

Five nautical miles from where Melanie and Wyatt were submerged, emergency sensors at UNCLE headquarters were tracking their route. The moment he had received the signal from Stuart's communicator pen, Don immediately called his team to inform them that "Sunday in the park" with their families was cancelled.

Alarms were going off in every corner of UNCLE headquarters. Every agent within a twenty mile radius had responded to the emergency call. Not a single one complained about having to cut short their one day off. The UNCLE network was stronger than any other ties. Nothing, not family, not friends, not even the birth of a child, was more important than the life of a fellow agent. They all knew that if any one of them were in a similar situation, every other agent would do the same for them.

No matter his suspicions, if Stuart was in trouble, Don was going to do whatever was necessary to come to his assistance. As soon as he received the signal from Stuart's pen, Don tried to contact his partner. He became very concerned when there was no response. It wasn't like Stuart not to respond, unless there was a really good reason why he couldn't. Don tried to put all of the really good reasons from his mind, even as it became more obvious as the time past, that there was only one reason why Stuart failed to respond, and that reason wasn't at all good.

Don's worst fears were soon realized when his lead agent Michael and the others who had been on their way to arrest Wyatt returned empty handed. They reported that they had arrived at Wyatt's moments after Melanie, and had seen Stuart enter the building along with several suspected THRUSH operatives. By the time they were able to infiltrate Wyatt's security, all they saw were dead bodies and the back elevator door closing behind who they assumed were the men who survived the blast.

"Carl reported that he checked Stuart's life signs but there wasn't any pulse," Michael said. "He was attempting to retrieve the body when the explosion shook the entire building. The subsequent fire was simply too intense for us, so we had no choice but to clear out. Sorry Don, I know Stuart was your partner for a long time."

"They'll be time to mourn his death later, Michael. Right now we need to find out who activated the communicator pen. We know it wasn't Stuart."

"We think it was your girlfriend, Melanie Tyler. We found her cell phone on the console."

Ignoring his personal comment, Don took the phone from the agent and immediately recognized it as Melanie's even before the agent confirmed the fact.

"We traced the number and it's definitely hers," Carl said. "But we can't figure out how one of our SIM chips got in there."

"We can ask her once we find her."

Don put the phone into his jacket pocket.

"And just for the record, she's not my girlfriend."

Yet

"But if she did set off the signal, that means she's on that sub with Gaynes and if that's true, she's in real danger, especially if those THRUSH agents are after him. She was working for us, so she's our responsibility. Get me the Coast Guard and one of our speedboats. We have a new mission, and this time I'm going solo."

Within minutes, Don was racing on the water following the blinking signal which was being received from the communicator's transmission. His could see Wyatt's submarine on his sonar in front of him and six other blip coming up fast behind him. He was painfully aware at how much distance there was between his speedboat and Wyatt's submarine. If anything happened to

Melanie, he thought, he didn't know what he was going to do to Wyatt, or anyone else who had put her in danger. He didn't want to think that the person who had put her in danger in the first place was himself.

Only a few hours earlier his biggest worry when it came to Melanie was how close she was getting to another man. Now, he was hoping that Wyatt was enough of "another" man to keep his lady safe.

His lady? Don shook is head. When did he begin to think of her as his? Was it when they first met when she smiled at him over the bar? Or was it when he was trying to teach her how to hold a gun and she had caught on so quickly? Or was it when she told him she was looking forward to seeing him at dinner and possibly dessert?

Don didn't know exactly when he started thinking about Melanie as more than just another operative but, he was absolutely certain that he would never be able to stop thinking about her if he wasn't able to rescue her before the other subs caught up to them.

He picked up his binoculars and scanned the lake with a spotlight, but everything seemed calm. Then, he noticed a small disturbance in the placid surface just ahead of him followed by the emergence of a yellow mini-sub. Don pushed the throttle so hard he almost broke the lever.

Had he turned around, he would have seen six other submarines also surface and begin to follow the speedboat toward the same destination. Under a minute later, Don was parked alongside Wyatt's sub. He drew his gun, kicked the hatch several times and ordered Wyatt to open-up.

Three seconds later, he did

When Melanie saw Don's face, it was all she could do not to jump straight into his arms. Instead, she calmly took hold of his outstretched hand, climbed out of the sub and onto the deck of the speedboat.

"How did you find us?"

She said, once she was safely on his boat.

"I followed the signal from your communicator pen. Once I saw the sub surface, I hit the gas, so to speak."

"Just like my knight in shining armor on the white horse I dreamed about, only your white horse is a white speed boat."

"Horses don't do that well on a lake, don't cha know," Don laughed. "I'd love to hear the rest of that dream, Mel, but right now I have a big fish to pull out of that little submarine."

Don reached into the hatch for Wyatt's hand, but Wyatt didn't move.

"I'm not going anywhere with you, Mr. UNCLE agent," Wyatt said.

"That's fine with me. I'm more than happy to leave you here to wait for your friends to catch up with you."

Don pointed to the mini-subs that were now only a short distance away.

"So, what's it going to be, Gaynes? You want to come with us and be safe or would you rather take your chances with your THRUSH buddies?"

Wyatt paused for a moment and thought about his options. He could decline Don's proposal and try and outrun his adversaries, but even if he managed somehow to get away this time, he knew they wouldn't stop looking for him and eventually would complete their mission. He trained them well. He still had a very large amount of capital in various accounts, but no amount of money would ever relieve the stress and worry of living a life on the run.

Realizing he didn't have a choice, Wyatt reached out his hand and climbed into the boat. As soon as he was on board, Don spun him around, handcuffed his wrists behind his back, then pushed him onto the bench.

"In case you didn't get the hint, Gaynes, you're so under arrest. You have the right to remain silent, and I suggest you exercise that right until I hand you over to my interrogation team."

Wyatt noticed that the submarines that had been following them were no longer visible. "What about those guys who were chasing me?"

"You mean chasing us, don't you Wyatt?"

Even with both their lives in danger, Wyatt was only thinking about himself, Melanie thought.

"We've already signaled the Coast Guard who should be able to intercept them sooner or later. For your sake, you'd better hope it's sooner."

Don turned the boat around and headed for Isle Royale where the rest of his team was waiting to escort Wyatt to UNCLE headquarters. Wyatt kept looking behind him to see if there were any signs of pursuit.

"Do you think I could get some kind of protection if I testify against them?" he whined.

"Oh, you'll be protected all right. As soon as we're done with you, I'm sure the Feds will be very happy to give you a one-way ticket to an undisclosed location as far away from here as they can find," Don said.

Once Wyatt was safely in custody, Don took Melanie back to the speedboat and they headed toward Abbeyville harbor. The Minnesota summer sky was crystal clear and covered with stars. Under normal circumstances a nighttime cruise on the lake would have been very romantic, but this cruise had been far from normal.

As if reading her mind, Don turned off the engine and let the boat drift. He sat on the bench next to her, put his around her shoulder and gazed at the stars. After awhile, Melanie felt comfortable enough to tell Don everything that had occurred from the time she had overhead the plot to kill Wyatt, till the moment she saw him looking down into the submarine When she got to the part about Stuart, she related his death and heroism in greater detail. She could feel him react with great sadness.

"Maybe if Stuart hadn't left Abbeyville in the first place, he'd still be alive," Don said. "He was the best partner and friend, I ever had, or so I thought."

"He did take the bullet that was meant for me, Don. He made sure I could contact you by giving me his communicator pen."

"Thank you for trying to defend him, Mel, but if it hadn't been for him..."

"If it hadn't been for him, you never would have known where I was and you probably wouldn't have arrived before Wyatt took the submarine into Canada. Stuart was my friend, too you know."

"Yes, I know. So was Wyatt. Should I always be on my guard when it comes to your friends?" he smiled.

"If you think the Abbeyville crowd is dangerous, wait to you meet my crazy friends in Hollywood."

The casual conversation was helping Melanie relax. She didn't want to break the mood, but Don needed to know one more thing.

"Right before he died, Stuart told me to tell you he was sorry."

For a few seconds, Don didn't reply. Then, he took a deep breath and said, "So am I."

Don pulled Melanie close to him. For a moment he wanted to forget he was an agent with the United Network Command of Law and Enforcement. He wished he was just an ordinary guy from Abbeyville, Minnesota.

Melanie relaxed into Don's warm embrace. His body felt amazingly strong and, for the first time since their adventure began, she felt totally safe. She turned toward him. Looking up at his alluring eyes, she placed her hand on the back of his head and lightly ran her fingers through his hair.

They were the only boat on the water, and they felt as if they were the only people on the planet. Melanie dropped the blanket from her shoulders, unfastened her bra and let the straps fall from her arms. Don kissed her lips, her shoulders and her breasts. His tongue continued its dance over her stomach creating shivers of heat that burned deliciously under his touch.

The boat rocked in the water with the rhythm of two people making real, honest and passionate love. Love making that wasn't an act, or an assignment, or a means to an end. They shared each others bodies, felt each other's hearts beat as one and, for the first time in each of their lives, allowed another human being into their soul.

Chapter Twenty-Eight

Back at UNCLE headquarters, Don was able to find Melanie a blouse from the undercover agent's wardrobe. She changed her top and waited, alone, as Don took Wyatt into the interrogation room. Whenever the front door opened, she half expected to see Stuart walk in, then she sadly remembered that he wasn't going to be walking into any room ever again. She hoped that someone from the agency would contact his sister and brothers and that they would tell them that he died saving her life and omit the part about him being the one who had put that life, and others, in jeopardy in the first place.

Melanie was exhausted. Even though it was just past nine, she felt her eyes close. Just as she began to doze off, Don entered the room. In spite of what they had shared on the boat, Melanie couldn't read anything in his expression. She had no doubt that he was well trained in concealing his emotions, even from himself.

"What's going to happen to Wyatt?" Melanie asked.

"Well, as you know, he successfully destroyed all the evidence we were going to retrieve from his operation. The very best we can hope to get him on now is blackmail and possibly false imprisonment, but those are pretty crappy consolidation charges next to conspiracy, counterfeiting and murder."

"Wyatt is still going to be prosecuted and go to jail. Isn't that what you guys wanted?" Melanie asked.

"Of course we wanted to put Wyatt away, but he has the names of over three hundred international operatives all over the world and we need that information more then we want to put him in prison."

"That sounds like a pretty big but for someone who is purportedly the head of an international crime organization."

"Wyatt thought he was going to be the head of the new THRUSH, but he really didn't understand why they failed in the first place, and why he never would have succeeded."

"Because you UNCLE guys are so much smarter?"

Don finally smiled.

"That's one reason. No, the truth is that Wyatt and THRUSH failed was because everyone in their organization wanted to be numero uno. Greed and revenge make men behave very irrationally. There is no trust when everyone is trying to step on everyone else to get to the top. Soon there isn't anyone left to lead and the entire system falls apart.

Wyatt had something we wanted, so we offered him the only chance he had to stay out of prison. He gave us the names and addresses of his entire network, and in exchange we're giving him a new identity. He's going into the federal witness protection program. He's been spilling his guts ever since we put in on the Coast Guard boat. He's in the interrogation room, if you want to see him."

"Why would I want to see him?" Melanie wasn't sure what Don was really asking.

"For one thing, once he goes into witness protection, you'll never be able to see or hear from him again."

"And that's a problem, why exactly?" Mel asked.

"You two have history," Don was trying to make a point. "After what you've been through, if you have any residual feelings for him you need closure, and you're not going to get another chance. You could compromise our arrangement with WITSEC. "

It was a great explanation, but Melanie understood exactly what Don was saying as to why he wanted to be certain that Wyatt was totally out of her life, and it had very little to do with UNCLE's arraignment with the U.S. Marshals Service's witness protection program.

"All right, Don. Just to ease your mind," she smiled, "I'll say my final good-bye to Wyatt."

"Michael here will take you to where we're holding him. I'll be waiting here for you when you're done."

Make it a quick good-bye, he thought.

Melanie followed the agent to the far end of a very long hallway. Under orders from Don, Michael stayed in the hall to allow Melanie to visit with the prisoner unescorted, even though the microphone and video camera were recording in case Wyatt said something incriminating.

It took Melanie's eyes a few moments to adjust to the dimly lit room. Once they had, she almost wished the room was even darker. She didn't want the last memory of Wyatt to be that of the person who was sitting in front of her in handcuffs. Wyatt's hair was disheveled, his face unshaven, the once proud egomaniac now looked completely defeated.

"Hi, Mel. I'm really happy you came to see me off. I hear your boyfriend is some kind of hero around here."

Wyatt smiled and for just one moment, looked like the high school sports star Melanie, and all the other girls in the class, had fallen for. But, it only lasted for a moment.

"He's not my..." she started to say, but it really didn't matter.

She was there to say good-bye to someone who had become nothing more than a fantasy of a time and place that never existed.

"Tell me one thing, Wyatt."

"Sure."

"Everything you told me in the submarine, was any of it real?"

"It was very real at the time."

"And now?"

"And now."

Wyatt looked up at Melanie. For a brief moment she saw a hint of his signature mischievous sparkle emanating from his gaze, but it was soon replaced by cold and lonely emptiness.

"We say good-bye."

Melanie walked over to his side, brushed her lips against his. Then she spoke the last line, of the last act, of the final performance of their three decades long two-character production.

"Good-bye, Wyatt."

Don was waiting for her when she left the interrogation room.

"Are you all right?" he asked.

"I'm fine, Don. Whatever Wyatt and I had, or didn't have, in fantasy or reality, it's been over for a long time and I'm finally over the over, if that makes any sense."

"Yes, it actually does," Don said.

"Witness protection will probably be worse for Wyatt then prison. A guy with an ego like his suddenly becoming a complete unknown? It's the perfect punishment. But, still I can't help feeling a little sorry for him. He thought he was going to take over the world, but he made a lot of bad choices."

"I'm just very relieved that you didn't get hurt."

Don put his hand on Melanie's and gave it a warm squeeze.

"You're still buying me dinner. The hotel restaurant is open late, and I don't know about you, but I'm starving."

"After what you've been through, I'll pay for the appetizer, dinner, and dessert."

"And breakfast?" she smiled.

"And breakfast."

Epilogue

The obituary that appeared in the Abbeyville Newspress reported that the brother of Jack Gaynes, Wyatt William Gaynes, was killed in an accidental fire at his downtown stationery store.

Even after his supposed death, Jack received top billing, and Wyatt's name was mentioned second. Jack led the memorial service which was short and sparsely attended. Brenda chose to stay home.

James O'Brien turned over all of his financial statements to the FEC, and after paying several thousands in fines, was completely exonerated. He re-introduced the bill to ban the toxic dye, which pasted unanimously, and his continued work on environmental issues further helped his political career.

James was offered the choice of running for Governor or U.S. Senate, but Katie made it quite clear that she neither wanted to move to Washington, nor have a part-time long distance husband. Eighteen months later, she and her family moved into the Governor's mansion in St. Paul.

Charles Haussman resigned from the Wall Street Journal and returned his Pulitzer to the prize committee along with a very public apology. He wrote a tell-all memoir of his experience with Wyatt and, after making several appearances on the talk-show circuit, his book soared to number one on the New York Times best seller list.

Eric Kramer had saved all the source codes and beta-test programs he wrote while he was working for Wyatt and he also kept all the prototypes Wyatt hadn't wanted. He moved back to Silicon Valley and founded a new software company which went public. Eric and his wife reconciled and they moved into a brand new home the week before their son's graduation from medical school.

After UNCLE closed the Gaynes case, Don transferred to the Los Angeles headquarters. With Stuart gone, he decided to take himself out of field work and instead train a new generation of agents, which gave him plenty of opportunity to make up for lost time in other areas of his life.

Melanie returned home and continued her voice-over career. She was happy to leave the spy business to the professionals, and more than happy to have one of those professionals share her ocean view condominium. When Don and Melanie married six months later, the guests on the groom's side of the aisle wore suits and ties. The guests on the bride's side wore shorts and t-shirts. None of the guests carried guns.

Walter Grant walked into the local bank in Barrow, Alaska to cash his meager paycheck. He looked at himself in the security video, and with the long, scraggly beard and fifteen extra pounds, even Wyatt didn't recognize himself.

He tried not to remember that day he and Melanie had been rescued from the THRUSH agents or the deal he had begrudgingly agreed to sign. Before the ink had dried on the paper, he had been placed into protective custody and flown to the farthest populated city on the North American continent. Even if he had managed to escape from UNCLE, Wyatt knew the international cartel would never have stopped searching for him. Had he gone to prison, his life would have been over within a week. He gave Don names, dates, locations, and in exchange, he'd gotten a one way ticket to the frozen tundra, as far away from civilization as they could send him.

Only months before, Wyatt had been moments away from realizing his dream, and just like that, it was all taken away from him. Now, everything was gone forever. For one shining moment, he thought he would be Mr. Gold, now he wasn't even Mr. Bronze.

Wyatt left the bank and walked through the slush in the street toward where he would be working for the rest of his life. He turned the key in the lock, opened the door and switched on the sign in the front window. Once inside, he picked up an iron and began pressing a pair of pants. The words on the sign lit up the dreary street in bright red neon: Del Floria's Dry Cleaners.

The End

Author's Note

Although this story is a work of fiction, the plot was based on factual events. In the last '60's my very best friend in elementary school and I were huge fans of the television show The Man From U.N.C.L.E. I did have a hidden room in my parent's basement, which was very much like the concrete room the characters were imprisoned in at the beginning of the story. The room was equipped with a lazy-Susan turn-table and stacks of files on two of our classmates who, for reasons forgotten long ago, didn't like us very much.

The idea for Undercover Reunion was born on the back patio of my girlfriend's home in Connecticut, where we were making the final plans for our 30th High School Reunion. She was, in fact, the chair of the reunion committee. I had brought The Man From U.N.C.L.E. board game with me, and while we were playing, we started talking about our classmates, some we hadn't seen since graduation, and wondered "What if?"

While some of the characters in the story may have been created from very old memories, they are all fiction. However, if there was a Wyatt Gaynes, I'm sure he would, indeed have an ego the size of Montana and a few small countries, but I highly doubt he would have aspired to be the head of an international criminal organization. Somehow I think he would have been much happier playing golf and ironing his shirts.

This book is dedicated, in memoriam to the following teachers of Ellenville High School

Anthony Croitz - English
Bill "Doc" Martineau - Chemistry
Mike DelGazio - Social Studies

About the Author

Raven West is the author of Red Wine for Breakfast, a behind the scene expose of Los Angeles radio and First Class Male, a romantic mystery involving a rural postmaster, a writer and a district attorney set in the majestic mountains of upstate New York.

West lives in Southern California with her husband William Westmiller.

Visit her on-line at http://ravenwest.net

44055359R00139

Made in the USA
Charleston, SC
13 July 2015